ASHLEY REYES

Honeymoon With His Brother

First edition

ISBN: 9798858752066

This book was professionally typeset on Reedsy.
Find out more at reedsy.com

To everyone on TikTok that made this book a reality, and anyone who believed in me.

Contents

Acknowledgement	iii
Chapter One	1
Chapter Two	9
Chapter Three	14
Chapter Four	17
Chapter Five	23
Chapter Six	27
Chapter Seven	32
Chapter Eight	36
Chapter Nine	41
Chapter Ten	44
Chapter Eleven	51
Chapter Twelve	56
Chapter Thirteen	62
Chapter Fourteen	66
Chapter Fifteen	70
Chapter Sixteen	75
Chapter Seventeen	77
Chapter Eighteen	83
Chapter Nineteen	88
Chapter Twenty	91
Chapter Twenty-One	96
Chapter Twenty-Two	101
Chapter Twenty-Three	104

Chapter Twenty-Four   110
Chapter Twenty-Five   116
Chapter Twenty-Six   120
Chapter Twenty-Seven   125
Chapter Twenty-Eight   129
Chapter Twenty-Nine   134
Chapter Thirty   137
Chapter Thirty-One   143
Chapter Thirty-Two   155
Chapter Thirty-Three   161
Chapter Thirty-Four   166
Chapter Thirty-Five   173
Chapter Thirty-Six   179
Chapter Thirty-Seven   183
Chapter Thirty-Eight   188
Chapter Thirty-Nine   191
Chapter Forty   195
Chapter Forty-One   202
Chapter Forty-Two   207
Chapter Forty-Three   213
Epilogue   216

Acknowledgement

This book wouldn't exist without my TikTok supporters. When I pitched the idea, people came running to me for the opportunity to read what I had written so far. I had people help with sentence structure, plot holes, grammar, and story structure. This book wouldn't be the same without Bri, Tiffany, Daisy, and Madisanne specifically. Thank you for supporting me, correcting me, and encouraging me. Without you guys, I wouldn't have finished writing.

Special thank you to my family for supporting me (here's that acknowledgment you requested.) I would be nothing without my sisters, Christina and Anya, and my parents. My brother, Tyler, is okay, too.

Chapter One

Hannah, Present Day

Looking at myself in the mirror, I was happy with the results of hours of work. My blonde balayage hair that fell to the middle of my back was tied up into a volumized updo with braids holding the hair back, and my face-framing bangs were in curled pieces on the sides of my face. I would've never imagined myself with my hair up, but the stylist said the style and volume she created would benefit my thin-framed face.

I trusted her as much as the makeup artist who said the cat eyelashes and brown shimmering eyeshadow would accentuate my blue, upturned eyes. Both of them were right. I looked like the bride I imagined I would. Gorgeous, and in a twelve-thousand dollar wedding dress designed just for me.

The dress I had designed was out of a dream I had. It was a sleeveless ball gown with a v-neck. The top was lace, and the royal train skirt sparkled with glitter. I loved how the style fit my thin frame, and the ball gown made me feel like a princess out of a fairy tale.

I was confused when I heard a knock on the hotel room door. All the bridesmaids were in the room getting ready, and no one from the wedding knew we were here. My bridesmaid, Nicole, let us use her room to get ready, so my husband-to-be couldn't find us and accidentally see me in my dress. Hearing the voice yelling from the other side of the door, I immediately recognized it as his. I became worried about him seeing me in my dress, which was why I came here in the first place. However, my worry was replaced with hurt and rage when I processed the words he said.

"Nicole, let me in. I'm sorry. You're right. We need to talk before I decide to go through with today," the man I was set to marry in a few hours pleaded from the hallway.

At first, I wanted to be angry with Nicole. Since she was involved in the wedding as a bridesmaid, she was someone I let close to me, despite my gut telling me not to. Someone who knew we were engaged couldn't use the excuse that they didn't know. She was at our engagement party when I asked her to be a bridesmaid, and she told us more than once how cute we were together. We weren't close, but as my best friend's cousin, I trusted her enough to involve her, and she broke that trust. But she wasn't the one who made a promise of commitment to me.

My anger shifted to my ex-to-be, the man who promised to love me through every up and down, proposed to me with a family heirloom, spent five years of his life with me, and believed in me despite his mother's harsh judgments when we first met - when I wasn't yet established in my career. He had years to tell me he didn't want me, but instead, he cheated on me despite asking me to marry him. I pursued Brad because I thought he was a safe option, but clearly, I was wrong.

I wasn't deemed good enough for their mom's dull investment banker son throughout our relationship, mostly because she wanted him to stay home and work with his father's company instead of traveling across the globe with me. In fact, she'd probably be thrilled to find out he had cheated on me. Unless she already knew, or worse, planned it.

I wouldn't put a stunt like that past her. With money and hatred, a lot of things were possible. Not that I'd know from experience.

I wasn't sure what happened between when he asked for the family ring a few years ago, and now, but I was glad I found out about it before replacing it with a wedding band. If he even planned to go through with it since he suggested otherwise when he thought he was talking to Nicole.

Instead of Nicole going to the door as he asked, I stomped to it and opened it to Brad Maverick with his jaw dropped and his eyes wide. He didn't talk for a moment as if he was trying to formulate a thought in his brain, anything, to get him out of this. His Yale education seemed lacking because while it may have made him a great investment banker, he didn't seem to have basic common sense.

Without thinking about my actions, my hand suddenly flung the mimosa onto his tux, which he was supposed to wear when we said our vows. It felt satisfying to ruin it. His mouth opened for a second, but any feeling besides guilt quickly faded from his face.

"Wow, you look stunning in that dress, babe," he said, stepping closer to me like I didn't just hear what he said. He seemed unphased by the ruined tux or the fact that he was dripping with my mimosa.

"You weren't sure you wanted to marry me when you asked me to marry you, dickhead?" I replied. I wasn't one to call someone a dickhead, but the name seemed fitting.

"I'm sure he wanted you before he had me back then," Nicole teased from behind me. She answered my question, but I was surprised she wasn't even trying to play the victim. She was proud to sleep with someone else's fiancé. I was ready to run to her and rip out the hair extensions that I paid for her to get for the wedding, but Priya, knowing me all too well, jumped in between us and held down my arms so I couldn't lunge for the bitch.

"Nicole, seriously, get the fuck out," Priya snapped. I knew she'd always pick me over her cousin, at least when her cousin was wrong. We had been friends since kindergarten, and Nicole was five years younger than us. They were related by blood, but our relationship had years more than theirs.

"Gladly," she said with her arms crossed around her chest as she stormed past us, "it's not like this wedding is happening anymore anyways, clearly," she spoke with a clear goal to strike my last nerve, and it was working.

"Baby," Brad said as he entered the room with his arms open like he was preparing for a hug and begging for forgiveness.

"Yes?" Nicole and I said simultaneously, looking at each other with thin lips and a cocked eyebrow. I wanted to vomit hearing her response to the name he called me, the name he must've also called her. Leave it to a math man not to be creative enough to come up with two different pet names. Or maybe he just wanted to make sure that he didn't confuse us.

He looked between us a few times, but his shit-colored eyes eventually made contact with mine, and he walked towards me. "I love you, Hannah; please marry me. We're so close. I made a mistake that won't happen again, I promise," he pleaded. I don't know why he thought I was as stupid as Nicole seemed. As if I would forget that minutes ago he tried to tell another woman he wasn't sure he wanted to marry me.

"That's not what you said last week, Brad. We'll be waiting for you at home when you come to your senses," Nicole said, rubbing her lower abdomen. Everyone audibly gasped before whispers started among the group. She was beyond embarrassing me at this point, but he was too. Thankfully, the room was only filled with my family and friends' and not Brad's. My people would side with me. Phones were left out of the room, too, due to the nature of my career. I couldn't assume something like this would happen, but I wanted safety just in case. At least this wouldn't be posted online.

"You cheated on me with someone eight years younger than you and got her pregnant? What is this, a midlife crisis at twenty-eight? You're sick, Brad," I spouted.

My anger took over as my face warmed. The champagne clouded my judgment and chose for me. I reached forward, my fist meeting Brad's harsh, chiseled jawline. If perfectly timed, his mom entered the room with his brother, Wyatt, pulling her sunglasses down to her nose. She'd be showing expression if she didn't have thirty years of Botox with fresh injections. She already hated me, but now she caught me punching her precious son.

"What the hell is going on here, honey?" she said, holding her son's freshly decked face as blood dripped down his nose.

"Your son cheated on me and got another girl pregnant," I said.

I knew she wouldn't care. She hated me. She hated that she deemed me unworthy, and Brad still pursued me. Unlike her, I had a career of my own, and I didn't need to rely on her son. She still didn't understand that and called me a gold-digger constantly. I met him when I entered college, and he was almost graduating, and we were both still nothing. He had no career, only family money, and I didn't know. He hid the fact that he had money from me. Contradictory, she told Brad I worked so much I couldn't possibly be a good mom to our future children.

"I'm glad you came to your senses about that girl," she said as if I wasn't standing right here, "but what will we do about the money for the wedding now? All those deposits are wasted. Because of Hannah's wedding demands, you'll have to work extra hard to make up that money."

"I paid for the wedding, you conniving b-" I started to spew at her, but Brad's brother, Wyatt, stepped between us.

"Okay, that's enough for one day. Mother, take Brad out of here, and don't let him return. I'm going to look at your hand, Hannah, okay?" he said, but I was too busy glaring at Brad to respond.

"We'll talk later, okay? I love you, Hans, and we can work through this," he pleaded as he trailed his mother towards the door.

"Don't. Don't call me or text me. I'll be busy in Florida with Wyatt accompanying me on our honeymoon." The minute the words left my mouth, I regretted them. Wyatt wouldn't go along with what I said, but I still looked at him with puppy dog eyes. We didn't exactly get along, he always found ways to tease me and make me feel inadequate, but I hoped he would realize how much I needed him now. He knew his brother was wrong for what he did to me, and I believed he wouldn't embarrass me.

"Yeah, I'll be keeping Hannah busy. Tell your girlfriend that I can perform her ultrasound when I'm back," Wyatt said with a wink.

I know he was throwing shade at his brother, but the comment hurt, and the reminder of his actions sobered me up too much.

"You've been screwing my brother?" Brad said with utter shock and disbelief as his mother dragged him into the hallway. You would never guess he went to an Ivy League school.

I wanted to lunge after the nitwit, but Wyatt could already read my mind. He placed a hand on either side of me, holding me tightly and looking me in the eye until my eyes met his. The same gorgeous soft, round eyes that I woke up to every morning, except for a beautiful hue of baby blue, and on his older brother. The doctor. The brother who deemed me not good enough, like his mom.

"Let me go, Wyatt." I struggled under his firm grip, but he only held me tighter.

"Let Brad go, Hannah. He's not worth it. Stay here, and I'll get some supplies for your hand, okay?" he asked, his eyebrows raised until I nodded in agreement, and he walked off.

Priya stood in front of me, her jaw dropped. "You didn't tell me you were going on your honeymoon with his brother, Hannah! You sneaky dog. Doesn't he know he's supposed to pick up a bridesmaid at the wedding, and not the bride?" she teased.

I put my forehead in my hand. Priya was gorgeous, but she wasn't always that smart, which was okay. "Priya, you were here the entire time. You knew I couldn't have planned that, seeing as I was marrying Brad today. It was last minute when I was heated, and Wyatt just went along with it. We're not actually going to Florida," I explained while shaking my head.

"I'm sorry, guys," I turned to face the crowd of family and friends who were surprisingly still standing there. "There's obviously no wedding today, and I prefer to be alone. I'm sorry," I said before walking out the door and down the hallway, unable to face anyone in that room yet. I had to stop at my room and get my stuff before leaving. I knew I'd run into Brad and didn't know what to say. Would he still plead to get me back, or would he be on his way to Nicole?

"Hey Hannah, wait," I heard Wyatt calling behind me. I stopped moving and waited in my spot for him to reach me with a bag of ice in his hand. "We have to look at your injuries. Come to my room while Brad packs," he urged.

I followed him to the elevator, up one floor, and down the hall. His room was bigger and nicer than ours, which wasn't surprising. He was a well-off doctor.

"Sit," he demanded as he nodded towards the bed. Something about the tone in his voice and the demanding energy made me immediately sit and look up at him. He grabbed an alcohol pad and cleaned my hand before putting ice on my knuckles. "You must keep this here for now to help the swelling."

I nodded my head. "Your room is so...neat. Organized, and all your things are still packed," I observed.

He laughed. "Probably a good thing now since I'm not staying here, obviously."

"Well, I'm glad my relationship falling apart can at least benefit you," I said with a small smile. Self-deprecating and dark humor were my thing.

"Look, about tomorrow," he started to say, but I shushed him. I wasn't delusional; I knew Wyatt wasn't going to Florida with me, but I didn't want to think about what that meant for me now. I had planned to take a few weeks off to celebrate my new marriage, but now I didn't have one to celebrate. I'd have to plan what to do for the next week, think about if I wanted to say fuck it all and go to Florida myself, and eventually, I'd have to figure out where I would live. The thoughts on everything that was changing sent my brain into a panic. I needed to get out and have a drink.

"Thank you for helping me, but I'm going downstairs to the bar. I need a drink or seven. I'm sorry about ruining your weekend date."

"I'm a doctor. It's what I do," he said. "I'll join you. It would be best if you had someone to keep an eye on you. I remember you're quite the partier when you're not upset. I don't want you to drink yourself to death just because you are." If that was what Wyatt truly thought of me, then no wonder he didn't want me with his brother.

"I forget that you were actually around for a lot of our relationship, and you've seen parts of me that I never realized. I guess I just thought you were never paying attention."

"I wasn't. I just heard Brad complain a lot," he retorted with a grin.

I balled my uninjured hand into a fist and hit him playfully on the arm for his remark. It was nice to see a side of Wyatt that was witty and joked around, different from the serious tone he often gave when we were around.

"Don't hurt your other hand now. I already fixed one," Wyatt teased. "Don't you want to change first?" he asked, looking me up and down as I was still in my wedding dress, but I shrugged and shook my head. I didn't care what I wore; alcohol tasted the same. Maybe the dress would earn me some free drinks.

I kept the ice on my knuckles and followed him out the door.

Chapter Two

Hannah, Five Years Ago

"Relax, Hannah. We can find you a cute outfit and still make you look sophisticated. You're good enough for him, and you're good enough for his parents." My roommate in my dorm told me. Stacy was friendly to me, even if we weren't close. She supported me, and she took me to parties often. Shopping was her thing, but usually, she found me slutty outfits. Today, my boyfriend told me his parents lived in Glencoe, a fact he left out in our three months together.

"I don't want to change myself to please his parents, but at the same time, I really care about this guy. I think we can have a future together," I explained my dilemma. It wasn't like I had only slutty outfits, but to families in his income bracket, appearance meant everything. My outfit and presence would convey a message, and I wanted mine to say that I was good enough for their son. He was everything I was looking for so far. When he invited me to his family's Thanksgiving, I knew he also thought about a serious relationship with me.

Stacy threw a matching set on my bed in my favorite color, pink. We were the same size, and the clothes came from her side of the closet. "Here, you can be a little bit of both," she said.

I held up the outfit. A pink blazer with gold buttons, a tight pink skirt that would land on my knees, and a white top to go under. It was cute,

9

totally something I'd wear, and an outfit that looked more presentable than anything I owned.

"It's perfect, thank you!" I said, jumping up and down. I had never had a serious relationship before. No parents to impress. No dinners with someone else's family. My nerves were on fire, and dinner was tomorrow. We didn't have time to do a full shopping trip like I would have if I had more notice.

"And pair it with these," she said, handing me a pair of white platform heels. They were undoubtedly cuter than my ten-dollar Walmart sneakers that I owned a few pairs of. Stacy, unlike me, came from money. I planned to pave my way and make my own money, so I was studying business, specifically digital marketing.

"What would you even do without me?" she asked, flipping her hair back. I rolled my eyes.

"Probably drink a lot less," I answered honestly, sending us both into laughter. She knew it was true, and she was proud.

"I'm out for the night. You know where I'll be. I'll see you after dinner, and you'll tell me all about it."

* * *

The next day, I arrived at his house early, prepared to hopefully make a good impression on his family. Brad told me his dad was coming to dinner, and he apparently wasn't known for being at dinners, even on holidays.

"Babe, you look absolutely stunning," he said as he brought me into his arms on his front steps. He hugged me tightly before interlacing our fingers and bringing me inside their gorgeous, large house. The inside was a pristine white, including the floor, and most decorations were a dark espresso brown. It was like a picture in a magazine, everything in an incredibly stunning condition — the complete opposite of what I grew up with. They even had living plants, which I never had.

"I'm nervous," I confided, as if it wasn't obvious. Brad dropped my hand and placed it on my lower back, urging me more into the house.

"Don't be. Why wouldn't they love you?" he said with a smile.

As we walked into the dining room, I bit my lip, trying to convince myself I was good enough for these people. His dad was on the phone, yelling at someone, and his mom was glaring at his dad.

"Gotta go. I'll call you later," the dad said as he hung up the phone.

"This is my girlfriend, Hannah," he introduced me, taking my hand in his. I smiled and gave a small wave, unsure of what to do.

I looked around the table at his family. His mom, dad, grandma, and a younger man around his age were sitting down. The man looked familiar, and it was hard not to notice that his eyes widened when he looked at me before they turned angry.

"Hi, everyone," I said.

"And this is my brother, Wyatt," he said, pointing to the younger man at the table. I reached out to shake his hand, but the anger on his face didn't change, and I took my arm back when he didn't shake it. Heat flooded my cheeks.

His parents had blank faces, so I had no idea what they felt, but I knew this man hated me. He just met me, and he didn't like me. What was I to expect of his strict parents if his younger brother didn't approve of me? Would they find me lacking as well?

"Brad, take a seat, darling. Hannah, you too. Tell us about you."

"Well, I'm studying digital marketing," I started with, and she visibly cringed.

"Where are you from? What do your parents do for a living?" She made it clear she was only interested in my net worth and class status. It shouldn't surprise me that my major did not interest her as, based on what little I knew of her, I had the impression she didn't appreciate a girl going to college. In her world, women were only good for making their husbands look good and bearing heirs.

"I'm from a small town in Tennessee, and my parents…" I tried to think of a lie, but I didn't want them to like a fake version of me. "My dad is in jail, and my mom was drugged out most of my life," I admitted. "I'm breaking a generational curse by going to college and making a life for myself."

Brad elbowed me in the side. I knew he wanted me to lie to gain their approval, but I couldn't. She became silent after that, and between her disdain for me and his brother's glares, I knew I was in for quite the night. I just hoped our relationship would survive this.

Once we finished eating with his family, Brad walked with me outside to send me home. He sighed as we stood outside, waiting for my Uber to arrive.

"Did you have to mention that shit about your parents the first time you met mine?" he asked with a bitter tone. I hadn't heard from him before.

"Either they accept me for me, or they don't," I explained, even though I felt he might be right. I could've held off that information, but Brad didn't properly warn me that his mother was that judgmental. "Your mother seemed to already have her mind intent on not liking me. Presumably because my outfit came from Kohls and not straight off the rack at some designer store."

He rolled his eyes. "She's not that bad, Hannah. She's my mother. You antagonized her by not even being friendly, then you talked about your sad family issues." My jaw dropped internally, but I didn't want to express my feelings. I didn't know he could act like this.

There was so much I wanted to say in response. Instead, I agreed. "You're probably right, Brad."

"Probably? Always am," he said with confidence. I hid my appall by smiling at him instead.

With one minute until my Uber driver arrived, Wyatt stepped outside.

He still had a straight face when he approached us.

"It was nice to meet you, Hannah. I hope you don't take offense to our mother. She'll never think anyone is good enough for her baby boy," he said, wrapping his arm around his brother's neck and giving him a noogie that made both of them laugh.

"Nice to meet you too, Wyatt," I told him, and he winced before he turned around and walked inside.

"I love you, Hannah. I hope you know all I want is for you to be the best version of yourself." Brad told me as I got into the car's backseat.

"I love you, too." When the car drove off, I couldn't help but think about how glad I was that Wyatt noticed how judgmental his mom was. For a moment, Brad almost had me convinced that I was overreacting. Brad may have sided with his mom, but I knew he loved me and just wanted his mom to accept me, which may have been easier if she had gotten to know me before finding out about my family situation.

Chapter Three

Hannah, Four Years Ago

I liked living with Stacy. She was quiet, relaxed, clean, and knew all of the good parties to go to. Since I had started dating Brad, I toned down the partying at his request. He made a point when he told me girls who plan to marry the men they're with don't go out drinking every weekend with their friends. I was serious about being with Brad and wanted to please him.

"This place is gorgeous, Han, seriously," Priya said as she brought in another box and set it down in the living room. "I can't wait to host a party here."

I laughed. "We can only afford it because Wyatt is living with us," I said with a groan. "Not sure why he'd want to live with me anyway. He's always so...quiet when I'm around. Broody, glaring."

"Maybe he holds a secret torch for you," Priya teased. One thing I liked about moving out of the dorms was living closer to my best friend, Priya. A few train stops away. It was hard to bring a guest into the dorms, so it would have to be at a party when we wanted to hang out. We didn't attend the same college. Instead, we had known each other since we were kids.

"You don't think this is a mistake, do you?" I asked Priya with wide eyes. I panicked about moving in with Brad after a year of dating, but I knew I was serious about him, so it felt like the right choice. Then he mentioned Wyatt moving in, and I panicked again. What would it be like living with the elusive Wyatt? I thought his asking me to get a place together meant he was leaving his brother behind.

"You're the only one that can answer that, sweetie. I love you more than I'll ever love a man, and if Brad hurts you, I'm prepared to cut his dick off." Priya smiled when she delivered that last line, and it was almost an evil grin.

"You're going to do what to my dick – and why?" Brad asked, setting down a box in our pile of boxes and walking over toward me, kissing my forehead. "Welcome to your new home, baby," he said. Wyatt and Brad already had this place picked out together and moved in weeks before me. Brad showed me the pictures, and there was no way I was going to say no to living in the neighborhood anyway.

"Cut it off if you ever hurt Hannah," she replied sternly, crossing her arms over her chest and making the 'I'm watching you' gesture. I laughed. Priya always had a goofy, fun attitude that rubbed off on me growing up. I toned it down for Brad, but if she and I were ever alone together, a different side of me would come out.

Brad made the point that I had to play the part now if I wanted to be an influencer on social media. I had to dress and act a certain way and be a role model for people. Eventually, every part of my life would be scrutinized by the internet.

Wyatt entered the room with a silent look and started moving my boxes to mine and Brad's room. Since there were two of us, we had the main bedroom. We decided on a king bed together. Brad's parents bought most of the furniture, except for whatever was in Wyatt's room. He wanted to pay his own way, while Brad was happy to accept his parent's money.

"I hope you don't mind, but I had a few outfits shopped for you by my mom's personal assistant," he said as he noticed me grimacing at the closet. It had several outfits that I knew she would've picked out if she could. It wasn't like I had to wear them often when I visited his family. Brad just wanted them to like me.

"No, thank you for thinking of me," I said, turning around and smiling up at him. "Always so giving."

"My mom offered, and I thought it was a great idea. I found your sizing from your old closet."

I held back the urge to roll my eyes. Of course, it was his mother's idea.

"Maybe when I get more followers and sponsorships and can travel when I graduate, she'll finally accept me as an equal."

"We're old money, babe. She'll never consider you an equal," he said with a chuckle, not realizing how he had hurt my feelings. But he was right.

"You're right," I frowned. "Let's go get dinner," I suggested. "We can bring Priya and Wyatt."

Chapter Four

E verything had to be perfect.

No one knew this was an engagement party, only that we were having people over to celebrate our new place. Right after he proposed, he suggested we buy a condo north of the city together. He was tired of sharing a space with his brother.

We had a condo within a few minutes of walking distance from Lake Michigan's pristine beaches. It seemed like the perfect place for us, even though I'd spend hundreds of days away each year. It was stunning and more spacious than Brad and I were used to in recent years. Not since before college, when we lived with our parents.

His mom despised us together, and so did his brother, so I was worried about how they'd react when they heard the news tonight. At least they'd hear the announcement over hors d'oeuvres and finely crafted cocktails. We hired a mixologist and a reputable catering company to make the night impressive.

I spent three-thousand dollars on a simple, elegant, off-the-shoulder red dress with a mermaid hem and a thigh slit. Brad had a matching tie with a tight-fitting black suit passed onto him by his father. He wore it whenever he wanted to please his mom since she loved it.

"Stop worrying, babe. You've improved over the years, and I think my parents view you differently. In fact, my mom said you're lucky to have me, and that's the nicest thing she's said about you." Brad said as he appeared behind me in the mirror, wrapping his arms around my waist. I kept quiet as I always did at his small jabs. They meant nothing. "And, of course, I'm lucky to have you."

"Guests will be here any minute," I reminded him, giggling as he nuzzled his nose into the crook of my neck.

"Everything is ready. The only thing missing is the people."

A knock on the door distracted our conversation, and I knew it was his mom. She had to be early for everything. She had to do her rounds and judge everything we had done.

"I'll get it. You just finish anything else you need to do," Brad said before running off. Our condo was one story, though large, and since our room was near the living room and entrance, I could hear him greet his mother.

I set the ring in my jewelry box to hide it until we had announced it and put on my mother's locket, the only thing of hers I had kept after she passed. I considered it my lucky charm and felt like I would need it to get through the evening.

I never had a close relationship with my mom. In fact, she's part of the reason I struggled with confidence and self worth, which was something I had to work on if I wanted to become an influencer. Part of me understood that I couldn't blame my mom for falling apart. Dad had ruined her, and he was rotting in prison for it. With him being in prison, she fell apart. She was free from him, but for whatever reason, she wanted him around. I wasn't enough for her growing up, and she became a shell of a person.

I took a deep breath and put on my biggest fake smile, walking out to be greeted by his mother's equally phony smile. "Carol, hello. Welcome to the new place," I said, bringing her into a small hug. I felt we both relaxed our faces each time we hugged.

"It's so...quaint. Reminds me of the first place Jeff and I had long ago, back when we were poor," she said, handing her jacket to a random catering waiter.

"Mom, he's not a butler. He's a caterer. And your poor was when dad made six figures before he made millions," Brad pointed out, taking the jacket from him.

"Same difference," she said. "And do you know how hard it is to live in an apartment?"

She acted as if the place she stood in wasn't a condo, essentially an apartment you owned.

"Oh look, more people," I said when I heard knocking again, walking to the door to leave the conversation. I could never tolerate more than five sentences with her. She was so insufferable. She smothered and spoiled Brad, and sometimes it showed too much in his personality.

Everyone else arrived quickly. It was only his mom, his brother Wyatt, my best friend Priya, and a few other friends that we wanted to impress. We had the type of friends who always liked to show off and kept people close for the sole purpose of saying they knew people. The relationships were shallow, but so was a party to announce our engagement in a way that cost thousands of dollars.

I waited until everyone was seated in the living room with a drink in hand before we decided to stand together in front of them.

"We have something to announce," Brad said.

"You're pregnant!" Priya screamed. I had never seen Carol's face look more disgusted.

"Heavens no. We're getting married!"

"It's about time," Priya said. "Personally, I think he took three years too long."

He laughed. "You think I should've proposed when we met?"

Priya stood up and wrapped her arm around me, pulling me away from him. "Of course, look at my best friend here. She's a babe, takes care of herself, and is well-educated." She left out how different I was back then. I wasn't this well put together in college.

I could see Carol roll her eyes before chugging her cocktail. I was sure that drinking would only make her speak her mind more, which worried me.

Carol was the first to get up and leave the room, announcing she was getting food, but I knew she didn't want to be around us anymore. Wyatt stomped out of there close behind her, a pained expression that I couldn't read on his face. Everyone else followed besides Priya, who stayed back to talk to me. I waved Brad off so I could be alone with her momentarily.

"I hope you know I wanted to tell you when he asked last week, but he told me not to. You can't exactly keep secrets very well," I said. Priya knew she had a blabbermouth. She never tried to deny it.

"I hope you know I'm the maid of honor, whether you like it or not," she said, placing herself in my wedding before I could even ask her. We both knew there was no competition for the position.

"Of course. You're my favorite best friend," I said, bringing her into a hug in which we squealed our excitement.

"I'm your only best friend, darling. No one else compares," she said. I loved her confidence in herself, and she was right. Every other friendship I had was simply superficial. "I just have one favor to ask."

When everyone walked away, I stayed to talk to Priya. She refused to ask her question in front of everyone else, which made me nervous.

"Hear me out. Will you ask Nicole to be a bridesmaid? It would mean so much to me."

I groaned. "You're lucky I love you." I never particularly disliked Nicole. There was just an age difference that made her harder to connect with.

I entered the parlor room where others had gathered, but Brad and Wyatt were missing.

Before I went off searching, I approached Nicole, sitting away from everyone, drinking a cocktail peacefully.

"Congrats, Hannah. I'm happy for you," she said, but something about it didn't seem sincere. "You're really lucky to have him." Something about her tone and phrasing sounded odd, but I ignored it.

"Hey, I wondered if you wanted to be a bridesmaid?" I asked.

"Yes, thank you for thinking of me," she said, her face still unchanged. I figured she was upset to see us being so happy because she mentioned going through a breakup with a guy she had been seeing for a while.

"Thanks, well…I'm going to find my fiancé now," I said, excited to call Brad my fiancé.

I walked down the hall until I heard talking coming from our room. They sounded angry, so I stayed back a bit to eavesdrop.

"I don't get why you can't just be happy for me," I heard Brad say.

When we announced our engagement, I noticed his face remained unchanged. But Wyatt hardly ever showed emotion. I had spent a lot of time around him since they had lived together, but I didn't know much about him because he'd hardly talk to me.

"You need to leave her; this needs to end," Wyatt replied. The words crushed my heart. It confirmed that he hardly spoke to me because he disapproved of me with his brother. I understood his mother's hatred of me - she thought no one was good enough for her son. Especially not someone who wanted to work and make their own way. She wanted someone who would stay at home and raise Brad's kids to be spoiled little shits. But Wyatt had no reason to dislike me. He had no reason to think I wasn't good enough, but he did. And the worst part was him judging me while barely conversing with me throughout my years with Brad.

I tried to move without being obvious, but I froze in place. I wasn't paying attention to anything until I saw Wyatt leave the room, his lips straight as he walked past me so fast I thought I would fall over from the wind he created. "Hannah," he said as he walked past, fleeing out the door.

His brother wouldn't stay for his engagement party. He disliked me so much that seeing me announce our engagement made him leave. Could I really marry into a family like this? One that didn't accept me? All of my life, I wanted to belong with someone's family, and Brad wasn't giving me that. But he said we could start our own family, and I counted on that. He said we'd be better parents than ours.

"Hey babe, I didn't realize you were here," Brad said. He had a nervous smile planted on his face. "Well, it went as well as we expected. At least Priya is happy for us."

"And you don't think it's a problem to get married when your family doesn't want us to?" I questioned with a frown. I wanted a sense of family due to not growing up with a legitimate one, but the fact that his family didn't like me took that off the table. I tried not to worry about it too much, since Brad said we'd make our own family one day. I wasn't sure if I wanted kids - at least not anytime soon - but the idea of children who loved me sounded nice. We'd make great parents and would right all the wrongs we were both given growing up.

Brad leaned into me and pushed me against the wall, pressing his lips gently to mine. "I love you, Hannah DeLayne, soon-to-be Maverick. Their pressure won't get to me. I won't allow it. I promise you."

I knew now that it was utter bullshit.

Chapter Five

Hannah

The hotel was expensive. The rooms were elegant, clean, and had high-end finishes. At four hundred dollars a night, I took a hit paying for everyone's rooms. On top of the hotel bill - which I already had a deal on - the drinks were atrociously expensive. I was on my third Captain and Coke, totaling sixty dollars in the first hour minutes we had been at the bar.

"Miss, are you Hannah DeLayne?" the bartender asked as I was about to order us another round of drinks.

I nodded my head. "Yes, sir, that's me. I'm Hannah DeLayne. I won't be Hannah Maverick like I expected," I replied, my words slurring. I wouldn't have said that last part if I were a little more sober.

"The manager has advised that you are a very special guest. He has requested I make you our signature cocktail and comp your bill if you post about us on your social media," the bartender offered.

"Yeah, of course." I wanted the free alcohol since I told Wyatt the bill was on me. He happened to still be on his first drink. Wyatt never was a big drinker, but tonight he chose to watch over me and kept his drinking to a minimum. I respected and admired his choice.

"Does this happen to you a lot?" Wyatt questioned.

"Sometimes a collaboration is established beforehand, but sometimes it is improvised, like this time," I said, hearing the slur in my words starting.

"Here you go, miss," the bartender said as he handed me this lovely blue cocktail that reminded me of the ocean. A cherry and a tiny umbrella garnished the side of the drink. I positioned it perfectly for my photo, threw on a filter over the image that brought out the colors more, and posted it with the hotel's location tag. I wouldn't be here long enough for my followers to come looking for me.

"All done," I told him with a smile. "Now it's time to drink it!"

"Are you sure you need another drink?" Wyatt asked.

I made direct eye contact with him as I started to swallow the drink quickly, stopping to breathe. "I don't need another drink, silly. I want one. Don't forget, I lost my fiancé like an hour ago." I played the emotional card, and he rolled his eyes. I could taste the rum in the drink, and it tasted like a sweet, delicious regret.

"You make it sound like he died," Wyatt pointed out, causing me to choke on the sip I was trying to take.

"I wish," I blurted out, blaming the Captain Morgan shots in my head. My comment made Wyatt chuckle. He was seemingly enjoying the sloppy drunk version of me.

"Come with me to Florida, for real," I suggested, wishing my mouth would shut up and stop speaking every thought that came into my mind. I didn't want to embarrass myself with further rejection from Wyatt, but I couldn't control my thoughts or speaking. The alcohol clearly clogged my common sense, too. As if I actually wanted to spend a week in Florida with Brad's brother.

"I don't think that's a good idea, Hannah," he said while shaking his head, but he had a slight smile peeking through. Of course, he'd reject my ridiculous suggestion.

I screamed excitedly when I heard Carrie Underwood's *Before He Cheats* come on the jukebox. I wasn't a fan, but I related to the song at the moment. "Come dance with me," I urged Wyatt. He shook his head and laughed at the stupid dance moves I was doing to entice him.

"I'm good. You shouldn't be dancing either, Hannah. You're drunk. You might fall and break a limb," he noted.

"Lucky for me, I brought my very own doctor," I said before running off to the area by the jukebox. He didn't follow, but he stared intently while he sat at the bar.

Only a few people were in the bar, but a girl dancing in a wedding dress must've caught people's attention because the men near me were staring. My head was spinning, or the room was, and I felt a burning sensation in my throat. I knew the overkill of alcohol was kicking in. I felt my limbs loosen on the dance floor, but I couldn't stop moving like I wasn't in control of my body anymore. It felt nice to let loose. And I felt safe with Wyatt there, which was an unexpected feeling. Wyatt may have slept around and expressed his disinterest in me previously. Still, he was being nice to me now and a serious, trustworthy person despite his extracurricular activities with women.

But apparently, I wasn't the best judge of character anyways.

"Where's the groom?" a man asked as he approached me, placing his hands on my waist. He was bold for acting like this, but disgusting to think he could touch a woman in a wedding dress or any woman who didn't consent. If I wasn't wasted out of my mind and prepared to pass out at any moment, I'd slap him.

Instead, Wyatt came rushing to my side with a face so serious you'd think someone had just murdered someone he loved. "Everything okay here?" he asked.

"Mind your business. Tell him that things are okay," the guy ordered. He must not have seen me with Wyatt before I came over here, or he had a death wish.

I couldn't form a sentence, so I shook my head, but the spinning motion made me sick.

"Wyatt," I drunkenly mumbled, unsure what I was asking for. He seemed to know since he immediately pounced into action and became protective of me.

"Get your hands off of her," he growled. "She's with me," he answered the man's question but didn't pretend to be my husband, which made the wedding dress more alien. The stranger eyed me up and down with judgmental eyes before deciding to walk away. Maybe it was the alcohol that made my cheeks flush and my brain have these thoughts, but Wyatt's defense of me was hot.

"I...I'm going to be sick," I said, fully prepared to throw up on the hotel bar floor, but big, comforting arms swept me up instead.

"You're awfully caring for someone that doesn't even like me. Why wasn't I good enough for him, Wyatt? Is it because my dad is in jail, or my mom is a druggie, or is it just *me*?" I realized I was rambling, but I couldn't stop. I heard Wyatt mumble, "If only you knew," but everything faded to black as he carried me away.

Chapter Six

Wyatt, Five Years Ago

Being a resident at an emergency room meant making time for friends and family was difficult. My brother and I lived together and we hardly spent time together. Since his school was ten minutes from my hospital, and I had just gotten off my overnight shift, I agreed to meet him for breakfast at his school. Usually, he got to campus early to take advantage of their free food before his early morning classes started. He also already paid for the campus meal plan, so it made sense. He also got a free guest meal, and I had to take free meals whenever possible. As a resident, I didn't make much.

I wasn't surprised to walk into a plate of bacon, eggs, and sausage, as I had texted him my order beforehand. I had only had a sandwich around midnight, so I was starving; therefore, I dug into my food before speaking to him.

"Good morning to you, too, brother," Brad said.

I finished my mouthful of food before responding, "thanks for breakfast, jackass."

We teased each other out of love regularly.

"Here, I got you some orange juice," he said, pushing the glass toward me. I started to chug it immediately.

"So, Mom told me to tell you you must be at Thanksgiving this year.

You haven't been in a few years."

I rolled my eyes. Thanksgiving was three months away, and I often got stuck working holidays since I was still a resident. Holidays are the busiest days of the year for us.

"I'll see if someone can switch shifts with me, but if she picks Thanksgiving, I won't be free on other holidays. She has to understand that as a doctor, I work whenever they tell me to and don't have the freedom of time off."

"Mom and Dad have to be the only two people in the world who could be disappointed in having a doctor as a son," he pointed out with a laugh. It was true. Our parents groomed us to work with our dad from a young age, instilling a love of math in us beginning in kindergarten. But as much as they tried to nurture a love for math, my passion for science won, which led to me wanting to become a doctor. I could help people and make a decent salary while I was at it. It was something I was good at. Though, I wasn't reaping the benefits yet. I was surprised I was even still trying at this point, with the shit money and rough hours, but I wouldn't give up and give in to what my parents wanted. I was my own person and in my mid-twenties, and it was time they understood that.

"At least you followed in Dad's footsteps, and now you're the beloved son, unlike me," I responded, teasing him. Mom always insisted she loved us equally, but she made it clear that she loved him more once he started to take after Dad.

"You were never the beloved son, asshole," Brad said with a laugh, shaking his head at me.

"It's not like we had a mom that came to our baseball games or brought us to the park, so how could she really show her love?" I replied. Mom always swore she loved us, but she didn't do much in terms of showing it. It was probably why we were both terrible at showing love, or accepting it.

"It's even weirder that she didn't have a job, so why did she need so many nannies?" I laughed after he made a valid point. We had rotating nannies, so we grew up with four different people caring for us.

"I'm going to go get a coffee. I think I need some if I want to make it home safe on the train," I said before getting up from the table and excusing myself.

The coffee and the mugs were out at a table for everyone to grab, and I poured myself a cup, adding a few creams and one sugar packet. I told myself that I wouldn't drink the entire cup, so I could get some rest during the day before returning in the evening. I liked working nights because you never knew what would roll in, but I hated that it took away my social life. Even in med school, I was a more fun person. I had a wild side. And my brother was there for it all, covering for me from our parents. Lying about where I was, my major, and everything.

I started to walk carefully back towards the table, weaving around eager students that weren't paying attention, but then a woman crossed my path carrying a few books and ran right into me. I was thankful that the coffee didn't splash on her, but it did soak a book she was carrying, which was now on the floor in a puddle of half a mug of coffee.

Happy Place by Emily Henry. I'd remember that, and replace it for her. It was the least I could do. I looked up to give her my charming smile, but I was met with cold eyes and a frown.

"That was my favorite book, thanks," she said.

I still couldn't help but smile at her. She was insanely gorgeous. She had straight brown hair that landed just below her delicate shoulders, and her cold eyes were a mesmerizing shade of blue. Her full, pouty lips were dying to be kissed. I was so stunned by her that I couldn't even speak, and before I knew it, she walked away furiously after she yelled at me a bit more. Even if I didn't know what she said, my biggest regret was not paying attention and asking her name.

I walked back to the table, sitting across from my brother.

"Smooth move, dipshit," he noted.

"I need to find her, Brad. I swear I'm going to marry her one day. You have to let me know if you see her on campus," I told him. "I'm going to find a copy of that book Happy Place she was reading, read it for myself, then find her and give it to her. I feel horrible."

Brad sat in silence as he shook his head with a smirk, amused by my blunder.

* * *

Three Months Later

When I first saw Hannah, I was attracted to more than her looks. She had many textbooks, which showcased her passion for her studies. She carried a fiction book, and I knew she liked to read. She had an attitude that challenged me to break through her shell. Now that she was in my dining room, eating with my family, I liked the attitude she gave my mother, too. She was fearless and confident in herself. She couldn't care less about what my mother thought - and neither could I.

I was furious when Hannah left. I was mad at myself because she couldn't understand why I was mad. She clearly didn't remember me, but a lot happened in those few minutes, and I couldn't blame her. Why would she have given me a second thought? Brad, however, didn't have an excuse.

"What the hell was that, Brad?" I asked when he walked back inside the house. My parents were around, and I didn't care. They hated to see us fight, and they already determined that they didn't like Hannah. She was beautiful, but they cared about money, status, and her ability to be a doting wife who would provide children and stay at home.

Hell, my father cheated, and my mother turned a blind eye.

"What is this about, Wyatt?" My mother asked with a sigh, sipping on her wine. Brad had given her stress by choosing to bring her here to meet them on a holiday. He knew what he was doing, too. He wasn't the kind to rebel or break the rules, but he sometimes pushed our mother's limits and tested her. I couldn't even tell if he really liked Hannah or if he finally wanted to rebel a little in his life.

"Ask golden boy," I said, my eyes not leaving Brad's.

"He's angry that he spotted Hannah first and didn't make his move. I got her instead," he answered with a smirk. So, he did know what he was doing when he brought her here. When he told me about her and refused to show me a picture, telling me simply that she was beautiful. I knew she was beautiful; I saw her first.

Mother rolled her eyes and sighed. "Two of my boys were into this girl? What's so special about her?"

"She's not just beautiful, Ma. She's smart, dedicated, loyal, trustworthy, and she believes in me," Brad answered, surprising me. I guess his feelings were genuine. "Her goal is simply to be good at social media or whatever, so I think she'll be fine sitting at home with the kids and scrolling on her phone or whatever." He was still a dumbass, actually.

"You boys are thinking with your dicks," my father chimed in.

"You forget that she's in my class. You knew this and still didn't try to talk to her. You left that stupid fucking book for her."

"Language, Brad," our mother warned. I tried not to chuckle. Sometimes, Mom treated us like we were children still.

"That book was one she clearly loved. It was a cute book, too. A romance story - something you'd know nothing about."

"Of course, you read the book she liked. You're such a sap. She wants a man like me, not one like you." Sometimes, I wondered if we shared any genes at all. Brad had clearly spent too much time with our father while growing up.

"Son, just focus on your studies so you can take over my business one day. Wyatt, don't you have a job to get to?"

"You guys made me take today off," I reminded. "Now I wish I didn't."

Chapter Seven

Wyatt, A Few Weeks Ago

Hannah left with Stacy, Priya, and some internet influencer friends an hour ago. She took a shot before leaving in an Uber, and Brad was concerned for her already. I rolled my eyes when he told her to be safe and watch her drinking because I knew Brad was about to get shitfaced himself.

Hannah had the idea of a bachelorette and bachelor combined party, but Brad wouldn't go for it. He was the kind of guy who believed it was his last day of freedom as if he hadn't chosen to commit to her years ago. I thought it was despicable, but I was supposed to have my brother's back over hers. He was family; in theory, family was always supposed to be there for you.

We all flew from Chicago to Nashville for the celebrations and rented a nice hotel downtown. It was Hannah's idea. Once Brad figured out how wild Nashville was, he agreed. Apparently, it was a common place to hold bachelorette parties. Hannah decided to go to a cutesy, pink-themed bar while Brad, his friends, and I were going to some famous country music bar downtown.

We entered a packed bar with hundreds of people. It was so crowded that we could barely move around. The girls here all looked similar to Hannah: long, blonde hair, pink outfits, and cowboy boots. While the guys seemed impressed by their options of women to take back to the hotel, I couldn't care less. I thought about it, of course, but lately, I have been sleeping with women less and less. My brother was getting married to the girl I loved, and I needed to finally try to move on and find someone of my own. I was older, yet I hadn't had a serious relationship since my early college days. And that ended horribly, with her leaving me for her professor.

It was only part of why I slept with girls but refused to commit.

"First round is on me," I announced to our group, and we headed to the bar. Most of us were whiskey drinkers, so I ordered a round of whiskey shots. Towards the back of the building, there was a stage where a country band played a blend of country and rock covers. They sounded good. I just hated how loud it was.

"No round is on me, fuckers. It's my party," Brad said. "Actually, hold onto this, Wyatt," he said, shoving his wallet at me. "I'll just get drunk and want to spend money."

"No round is ever on your cheap ass, Brad," his co-worker, Steven, said. He patted him on the back. "We're still your friend, though."

"Yeah, because I'm the boss's son, you kiss ass. You know I'll take over one day."

"Well, duh, Brad. You didn't think it was your charming personality, did you?" Steve joked, handing him another shot of whiskey. "Now, let's get this night fucking going."

Steve handed everyone a shot, and then we sat at a booth towards the front where the music was a little less loud. A group had just walked away from it, so we got lucky. A server brought us shots, and Brad was wasted in less than an hour. He, his friend Steven, and one of his college friends, Matt, walked to a table of girls together, leaving me with two of his friends behind at the booth. I was surprised he was so boldly flirting with a girl, but at the same time, I wasn't surprised at all. Brad had an untouchable attitude, even with his fiancé a block away.

One of the girls leaned into Brad, and he didn't push himself away. Instead, he leaned into her, and I watched as they kissed. I felt disgusted by his actions. I knew men often thought it was their last shot at freedom and that they were supposed to make out with girls and watch strippers, but it was an archaic routine. One that I refused to participate in when I did decide to marry someone one day.

"Tell Brad I got a headache and went back to the hotel," I said, rolling my eyes as I stood up from the booth. I downed two shots before leaving to drown out my guilt. Our hotel was close, and I felt like walking to clear my head. I knew so many of Brad's secrets, secrets that hurt Hannah, so how could I look her in the eye? How could I watch her marry him? Brad would make me feel guilty whenever he fucked up. He'd tell me that we're brothers. We watch each other's backs. He'd remind me of the times in high school when he'd sometimes take the blame for me before I got my shit together. By now, I thought he was right. I was ashamed.

My room was next to Brad's, and since I had Brad's wallet, I somehow ended up in his room using his key card. The drinks must have started hitting me on my walk. I was so tired when I ended up in the room that I decided to lie down on the bed. I heard a woman groan next to me, but it was dark. The only person it could potentially be is Hannah.

"Brad?" she said sleepily.

I froze. I wasn't Brad. Hannah was in bed with me. Now, she was facing me, but it was so dark that she couldn't see me. I knew she couldn't because if she could, she wouldn't have grabbed my face and leaned in, kissing me while wrapping her legs around my waist. Her kiss was soft and heavenly, but she thought I was someone else. The way her lips felt against mine hit me like a drug. She tasted sweet like orange juice and vodka. I needed to put a stop to this before she regretted it more. Before she remembered what happened in the morning and hated me. At the same time, I was mesmerized and lost in her kiss, knowing it would never happen again.

I tried to pull away but her hand landed in my hair, pulling my face closer as her tongue ran along the seam of my lips. Then she pulled away, likely realizing I wasn't Brad when she felt my hair. She jumped from the bed and turned on the lamp.

"Wyatt?" She looked at me with wide eyes, standing still in her place by the wall. "Why the hell are you in my room, and where is Brad?" With the way she looked at me you would assume that she thought I had just murdered him. I thought about it. Not in a literal sense, obviously, but sometimes he drove me crazy. I had no idea why I still defended him sometimes.

I tried to feel bad about not breaking that kiss when I should have, but I couldn't after watching Brad kiss someone else. I stood from the bed, re-making the sheet on my side. "I have his wallet and accidentally used his key to get in here," I admitted, then I fabricated a lie to get out of the second half. "And I thought you were a girl I had sent to wait for me." I set Brad's key card on the table. Hannah stared at me, blinking a few times, seemingly unsure of how to respond.

A knock on the door interrupted us. A drunk Brad was on the other side, slurring his words. I opened the door and caught a stumbling Brad before he fell. "Easy there, buddy."

"What are you doing here?" he questioned, looking at me with furrowed brows.

"I had your wallet and accidentally came here instead." I handed him his wallet back, then took one last look at Hannah. Her expression looked pained. "I'm going to go. I'll see you guys tomorrow."

Chapter Eight

Wyatt

I thought about not going to the wedding. I promised my brother I'd be there, but he knew what it meant to me when I made that promise. After years without even living with them, I felt like I shouldn't have any remaining feelings towards her. She was my brother's fiancé, and it was my fault I didn't make a move sooner.

On top of that, I thought that living with her would make my feelings disappear. I figured being close to her constantly would make me hate her bad habits, like how she left her socks all over the place or forgot to lock the door often. Sure, some of the things she did annoyed me, but I didn't care. The way she sang when she thought no one was around and danced in the kitchen when she thought she was alone made me happy. I saw the bad, but I was forced to see the good, too. Brad took all of that for granted consistently.

I even made plans to bring a girl. To help myself feel more relaxed, and to convince my brother that I had no feelings for Hannah. Send a message that I was happy for their marriage, even if it was far from true. Something inside me told me it was wrong, and I canceled on her. Instead, I booked myself a hotel room for the weekend alone. I never took vacations and couldn't go far, so a weekend getaway in my city was perfect.

When I saw Brad roaming around the place, I decided to follow him. He wouldn't have been trying to see his fiancé. He knew she thought it was bad luck. He wasn't walking towards the groom's suite, so where the fuck was he going? I was surprised when he stood outside a hotel room I knew didn't belong to me, her, or Mom. But then he spoke, and my surprise turned to burning rage. He was still seeing her after all this time. He was betraying his fiancé on their wedding day.

My anger turned back to surprise when I heard more voices inside. Hannah was in that room. Brad went in shortly after, and I followed him in. Things were so tense that no one noticed me until I had to stop Hannah from pissing Brad off more and get her away from him. Her hand was injured already. I had to listen to my mom spew bullshit at Hannah, who did nothing wrong, but I wanted to rip into her. It was Brad's job, though, and he failed.

So when she told the room she was going on her honeymoon with me, in her attempt to make Brad jealous, I agreed. I knew she wouldn't really want me there, but we could make everyone think so. I took her side because while he was my brother, he was in the wrong.

When I took her back to the room and helped her care for her hand, I realized that my feelings for her still lingered, and I was reminded of things I liked about her. I liked the way she fought against Brad, the way she didn't go right back to him, and the way she never tolerated my mother's behavior. She had a fire in her that couldn't be extinguished, but he threw the water on the flames for years.

When she announced that she wanted to drink, I decided to go along with her to protect her from herself. She downed shots quickly and started dancing, and with the way men looked at her, I was glad I came along. Hannah was drunk and upset, and I wouldn't let anyone hurt her. What fucking idiot hit on a girl in a wedding dress?

Then, the idiot touched her, and she mumbled my name. I breathed a sigh of relief before

"Get your hands off her," I said with a voice of anger that I didn't recognize as my own. The stranger looked between us before throwing his hands up in surrender and walking away. I was glad the fight went nowhere.

Immediately after he left, she looked ready to faint, so I scooped her into my arms and brought her back to the room while listening to her drunk ramblings that made me chuckle. One day, she'd know the truth. If I told her now, she wouldn't remember in the morning.

Hannah looked so peaceful while passed out in my arms. I carried her toward her hotel room. Hopefully, Brad was gone.

"Wyatt," Hannah mumbled against my shoulder, her arms draped loosely around my neck. The way she said my name with a rasp made me smile. "Maybe I was about to marry the wrong Maverick brother," she said. My heart skipped a beat. I heard her correctly, but I couldn't believe her subconscious words. She wouldn't remember it in the morning, but I would.

I decided to change my route and brought her to my hotel room. I wanted to go to Florida with her, and I didn't want her to wake up in the room she shared with my brother. If I didn't go with her, she could meet and fall in love with someone out there. I needed to show her that I was an option. That I care about her. That she can have fun with *me.* Some part of her mind clearly had some thoughts about me, too. Most importantly, I needed to show her that I never hated her. I never thought she wasn't good enough.

My biggest fear was that she'd wake up and decide she still wanted to marry him.

Once we returned to the room, her consciousness returned, only for her to rush into the bathroom and fall to the floor by the toilet. I knew she was about to puke, and I held her hair behind her head to make sure she kept it free of vomit. I had never held a girl's hair and watched her throw up before, yet I wouldn't have wanted to spend my night any other way. Because the alternative would be my head in the toilet if things went differently.

"I'm sorry," she slurred her words into the toilet. After wiping her face with toilet paper, she flushed the toilet, and I offered her my hand to help her stand.

I walked out of the bathroom and grabbed a plain white shirt and a pair of boxers, the only things I figured she could wear. She presumably didn't want to fall asleep in a wedding dress.

She looked like she was trying to slip it off but struggled, so I helped her zip it down, take it off, then helped her slip out of it. I kept my eyes respectfully on her face, then threw the shirt over her head, helped her arms into it, and helped her step into the boxers.

"Bet you're used to slipping girls out of their clothes," she said. I chuckled and hoped she'd forget everything she said in the morning.

I picked her up and carried her in my arms, setting her down on the bed. I had booked a king-size bedroom, even though I expected to be alone. It would be big enough to fit both of us and give us space. When I tucked her into the blanket, her eyes instantly shut. With her asleep, I decided to pack her stuff. I grabbed her purse, found her hotel room key, and headed to her room.

I heard voices before entering the room and knew Brad was there. I was disgusted when I heard Nicole's voice mixed with his. I was more disgusted when their voices stopped, and I opened the door to them kissing against a wall, the lights dim.

"Hannah?" Brad said eagerly before I fully turned on the light, and he turned around. He was disappointed to see me in her place.

"I'm here for her things," I explained. "You know, Brad, I'd deck you in the face right now for what you're doing, but I think your *ex*-fiancé got that covered today." I smirked when I saw the forming bruise on his face. I loved my brother. How could I not when we grew up together, and blood bonded us? I didn't always like him; right now, the dislike overpowered the love.

I started to walk into the room. Hannah's bag was on a chair, and some of her stuff was scattered. It looked like a wreck. I took everything out and started to pack things more neatly and organized, going between the bathroom and the bedroom.

"Where's Hannah?" Brad asked, Nicole still at his side.

"In my bed," I said, offering no further explanation. "And you will leave her alone, or I will punch you. You didn't even try. Here you are with Nicole, the girl you cheated with."

"*One* of the girls," he clarified. Every time he opened his mouth, he dug a bigger hole for himself. I finished packing her suitcase and zipped it up, putting it on its wheels and popping up the handle. "I'm going to bed, then I'm going to Florida. Then, next week, I'll come to check out your baby. The one you're having without your fiancé."

"Just...just tell her I'm sorry," Brad said softly.

I opened the door, setting the suitcase outside. "If you're sorry, then leave her alone. The damage is done. Clear this hotel room and move on with your life."

Chapter Nine

Hannah

I awoke to an obnoxious alarm that exasperated my raging migraine and turned it off. When I looked at the clock, I realized it was five in the morning, I wasn't packed, and I didn't think I was in my own bed. I wasn't even dressed in my wedding dress anymore. When I took off my blanket and looked down, I noticed I was in boxers and a shirt.

Oh no, what did you do now, Hannah? I thought to myself before turning around to see Wyatt sleeping peacefully next to me, making the entire situation worse. Wyatt Maverick was the last person I wanted to drunkenly hook up with and wake up next to. I felt a new wave of sickness as I stood up from the bed and ran to the bathroom to hurl in the toilet.

"Are you alright in there?" I heard Wyatt ask groggily.

"Yeah, just great," I responded sarcastically, as if it wasn't apparent that I wasn't doing well.

"Has anyone mentioned you might have a drinking problem?" he questioned with a chuckle, appearing next to me seconds later while I had my head in the toilet. "Here, drink these," he said, handing me a cup of water and a mug of coffee.

"Thanks, has anyone told you you are an asshole? Now get out. This is so embarrassing," I said.

"Not after I've kindly handed them drinks to help them with their hangover." He chuckled. "I already witnessed this last night, held your hair back, and dressed you in my clothes."

"That's worse. We didn't..." I started to say, and he knew where I was going, violently shaking his head.

"God no, Hannah. You were obliterated. I wouldn't do that to anyone, especially not you."

Not because he cared but because I was formerly, somewhat currently, engaged to his brother.

"After I put you to bed, I went and packed your things. You'll be happy to know that all Brad's belongings are gone from the hotel room, and you don't have to see the room again," he said.

"You grabbed my things for me?"

"I hope that's okay. I wanted you to sleep in. Your flight is at 8, so I set the alarm for good timing."

I nodded my head, flushed the toilet, and stood up. "Thank you." I walked to the room to go through my suitcase and look for Advil, clothes, and my toothbrush. "Wow," I said, looking at the meticulously packed suitcase. My hygiene products were in a bag in the corner, my clothes were neatly folded, my first aid medications were together, and my socks were bundled together. All things that I never did myself.

"I know you usually keep your stuff chaotically organized, but I just went for normal organized."

I didn't know he paid attention to anything about me.

"What do you mean?" I asked him to elaborate.

"Your things are a mess, but you know where everything is," he explained, and I laughed. It was true. I could tell you which junk drawer something was in or which notebook to look for in the stack to find a particular note. I didn't organize any of my stuff unless it was work-related and I needed easy access.

Shocked at the revelation that Wyatt knew anything about me, I took a moment to study him. I had to admit that even after just waking up, he looked gorgeous. His brown hair, usually pushed back, had fallen to his eyebrows, and looked just as good. He had more facial stubble than Brad, which suits him better. While they had the same hair color, straight nose, thin lips, and even the same high cheekbones, I was shocked at how much they didn't look alike. Beyond just their eye color, Wyatt's hair was straight, while Brad's short hair was always curly.

He certainly had more style than Brad, whose outfits always said, "Do you know who my father is?"

As I walked towards the bathroom hallway, I noticed Wyatt's bags in the hallway and turned to look at him. "Why are your bags here?" I questioned.

He grinned. "You invited me to Florida last night and told a dozen people we were going together, didn't you? You said a lot last night, actually," he teased, hinting at something I knew he wouldn't let me live down, but would also keep from me until the perfect time.

"I also drank so much that I puked, so I clearly wasn't making good choices last night. I don't suppose you will tell me what else I said?"

"Don't worry. One day, I will." He winked.

I rolled my eyes. "I'm going to shower and change," I said, walking off into the bathroom, locking myself in there, and turning on the water to let it get warm. I stared at myself in the mirror while waiting, wondering how the hell I got here. I felt like crying, but I also felt like I had no tears to shed. I knew it would hit me eventually, but now I needed to get ready for a vacation I had to spend with the brother of the man I should be married to and traveling with. If Wyatt didn't change his mind while I prepared.

Chapter Ten

Hannah

Brad and I planned this honeymoon together, and now he wasn't here. It was too late to change my course since some of the stuff I booked was non-refundable, so I figured it would be worth it to go. Maybe being in the sun and feeling the sand between my toes would cheer me up. We weren't staying on a beach, but they were close enough that I'd be able to visit one.

Waiting for the shower to warm up, I looked at myself in the mirror, twirling the ring on my finger as I thought back to the day he gave it to me. A day I've come to regret.

* * *

Brad said he wanted to take me to this new restaurant in town. We made a dinner reservation for Saturday at seven, and I had a gut feeling he was going to propose to me. He wasn't one to get dressed up and go out to dinner with me often. At least, not dinners that are thousands of dollars.

The minute we walked in, Brad ordered us an expensive bottle of champagne, and he ordered us appetizers, entrees, and dessert. The restaurant had a romantic feel to it, most tables only seated two, and the lights dim. There was even a piano player in the corner of the room, which I thought was something only seen in movies.

After about an hour between arriving and finishing dinner, I figured we were ready to leave. Then, Brad fumbled around in his pocket, and my heart rate increased. I wondered if he was looking for a box. He was sitting across from me at the end of the table, but he moved from his seat and kneeled in front of me at the end of the table.

"Hannah DeLayne, I have wanted you since I first saw you, and I have loved you since I first met you. I want to provide for you for the rest of my life and start a family together. I want to do everything with you forever. Will you marry me?"

Most girls cried when they got proposed to, but I went wide-eyed and smiled, happy by the moment but not brought to tears. Marriage was something we were always heading towards. It was what serious couples did, and I didn't find it particularly special enough to cry.

"Yes, of course, Brad," I said, accepting the ring and letting him place it on my finger.

"Whew," he said with a sigh. "Just promise me one thing. When we honeymoon, it'll be something simple. Florida. My favorite place. I want to know that those followers didn't get to your pretty little head and make you pretentious."

* * *

I should've known he was a walking red flag back then. Who the hell said that to someone after proposing to them?

"Are you alright in there?" I heard him ask from the other side of the door.

"Yeah, why?"

"I've heard the shower going for five minutes now, but I still see your feet by the door," he responded.

"Stop trying to spy on me from the crack under the door, perv," I said as I slid off my clothes and hopped into the warm, refreshing, and invigorating shower.

I used my fifteen minutes in the shower to cry until Wyatt started knocking on the door and asking for his turn in the shower so we could leave for the airport. "Just a sec," I shouted, hoping my voice didn't sound too shaky, and he couldn't hear my sobs over the stream of water.

I threw on clothes I planned to wear on the flight, braided my hair, brushed my teeth, and threw on some deodorant before leaving the bathroom.

"Finally," he said as he raced inside.

I looked at the clock, realizing it was only five twenty, and he had no need to rush. I could've still cried for a few more minutes if he hadn't interrupted me.

I made sure all my things were packed, and my suitcase was closed before I set it on the bed, ready to leave. One thing was still hanging up and staring at me: my wedding dress. It had stains from spilling alcohol and food last night when I got sloppy drunk, but it was still hung neatly in the bag it came in, something I assumed Wyatt did.

"So, what are you going to do with it?" he asked, coming out of the bathroom with a towel around his waist and his hair wild from the water and towel drying. I wasn't used to seeing him like this, and I bit my lip as I looked at him. He was attractive, his muscular upper half glistening from the water still on his chest and arms. Looking at his body distracted me from answering his question.

Despite being around him often, I had never seen him shirtless. Seeing him now brought butterflies to my stomach and redness to my cheeks. I could tell by the smirk on his face that he knew exactly what he was doing.

"Sorry, forgot my shirt," he said, grabbing one from the drawer.

"I think I'm just going to leave it here with a note to toss it in the dumpster. I don't want to look at this dress ever again," I replied. "Now, go put a shirt on and some pants while you're at it." I shook my head while watching him return to the bathroom with the door open.

"I'm not used to women saying that," he returned with a chuckle.

"Your shower was so fast that you didn't even need to rush me out of there."

"If I gave you too long, I was afraid you would drown in your tears," he responded.

He walked back out of the room in jeans and a shirt. I had hardly seen him without a suit before. He wasn't the type for casual outfits, so this was surprising.

"What are you staring at?" he questioned with a smirk.

"Even at family dinners and holidays, I'm not used to seeing you in casual clothing," I remarked.

"Vacation doesn't require suits," he said in a serious tone.

"And eating turkey at a table does?"

"Grandma visits, and she likes everyone to dress their best. It's respectful to the family and guests, she'd always say."

Not having anything else to say, I picked up my bag. "We should probably catch an Uber," I suggested, walking out the door without looking at him.

The ride to the airport wasn't bad at five-thirty in the morning, but the airport was packed with people traveling out of the state in January. Our flight to Florida had many people, but I noticed people running off to flights to California and Arizona to escape the Chicago cold.

We got through security with thirty minutes to spare before boarding and headed towards a cafe together. Wyatt first walked up to the counter, and I assumed he'd order for himself.

"Two dark roast coffees, please, one with two packets of cream and one sugar," he ordered. He obviously wasn't drinking two coffees to himself, and one of them perfectly matched my coffee order.

"How did you know?" I questioned, perplexed by his ability to order my coffee.

"I pay more attention than you think, Hannah. I just don't always show it," he responded. It was the hottest thing I ever heard, given that Brad still didn't know my coffee order after years together. I had to text it to him every time and bring my own coffee materials when I slept over.

Our coffee took a few minutes, and then we walked to our boarding area and sat and sipped our coffees without exchanging words until we heard the announcement for our boarding.

I got up from my seat and walked to the line with him behind me. We were close to the front, meaning we'd get a good choice of seats.

"Window seat or aisle?" Wyatt asked me. I was shocked to be given a choice. Brad refused to sit near the window, which was good for me, but it never sat right with me that I didn't get a choice.

"I prefer a window so I can take photos for my social media, but if you want it, that's fine," I answered.

Wyatt chuckled. "Of course you do," he teased.

I crossed my arms, looking at him with a raised eyebrow. "You know it's my job, right?"

We showed our boarding passes and walked down the hall and into the plane, sitting in seats in the middle. I threw my bag under the seat in front of me, and so did Wyatt. He took out a book, and I threw on a sleep mask. I couldn't see, but I could hear him laugh.

"Going to bed on our flight?" he asked teasingly, something he was great at.

"I'm hungover as hell, and I'm scared of flying," I admitted.

Despite not being able to see his reaction, I imagined what his face looked like now. He was grinning, knowing a fact about me that few understood. I tried to hide it from Brad, and I hid it from my millions of followers.

The plane started to take off, and I felt the terrifying feeling of ascending, gripping the arm of my seat. I felt Wyatt's hand over mine in a comforting way, but I didn't take off my sleep mask or open my mouth to say thank you. He knew I was scared, and he was trying to comfort me.

"It's okay. Only a few hours left, but at least we'll be flying straight soon."

"Good. Now you just have to prepare to comfort me when we start descending." I smirked, partially glad that I couldn't see his face.

"I'm ready," he assured.

* * *

After a few hours, we arrived in Florida. As promised, he held my hand during the descent. I only opened my eyes to take a few pictures when we were cruising at the same altitude. Once I put my sleep mask away, I edited the photo and put it on all my social media platforms. Then, I turned off their notifications so I wouldn't be bothered by them pouring in while I was traveling.

My followers would expect wedding content soon, and I wondered how quickly I should be open with them. It wasn't their business, but I made my page about transparency and honesty and needed to provide that.

"When we get to the hotel, I have to release a video statement about what happened," I said as we walked down the aisle to get off the plane.

"Understandable," he said, surprisingly. He seemed like just another man who didn't understand my job of social media and traveling.

"Thanks for saying that."

Stepping outside the airport was a breath of fresh air. I felt the sun beat down on my skin and the air entered my lungs.

"It's nice here," Wyatt said.

"Have you never been to Florida?" I questioned.

He shook his head. "No, never. I went to medical school, worked at the hospital for residency, then started working at Dr. Miller's practice."

He had access to all the money he could ever imagine, but he left the family business and went to medical school instead. It was impressive. If I were in his shoes, I wouldn't have gone against my parents' wishes when they offered me money to not become a doctor.

I was glad they pressured Brad into school for accounting, but not anymore, given that I met him there and regretted meeting him at this point.

"Well then, I suppose I have a lot to show you in Florida," I said with a beaming grin, following him into our scheduled Uber.

Chapter Eleven

Hannah

Walking into the hotel was nerve-wracking. I knew they'd assume Wyatt was my husband and that we were going to stay in a one-bed hotel room and do things together as a couple. I'd have to tell them that I didn't get married and he wasn't my husband. Then, I'd face their judgment. I'd judge me too if I didn't know me, and I showed up to my honeymoon with a different man.

"'Hi," I said to the smiling redheaded woman at the check-in counter, "I'm here to check in for Hannah DeLayne," I told her.

She asked for my ID, and I handed it to her.

"The honeymoon suite for two for our travel blogger and her new husband. Fully comped as long as you two post content and hold up your end of the contract," she advised with a smile.

I thought back to the contract I had signed with the hotel. I didn't ask to be fully comped, but they offered it in return for posting on my social media feeds, social media stories, and an overall travel blog post when I returned home. The contract I signed was based on my honeymoon with my husband, and now, there was no husband.

"That won't be an issue," Wyatt intervened, elbowing me in the side. "We're happy to be here and celebrate our new marriage. Thank you for the generosity."

Before I could respond, he put his arm around me and pulled me to him, and she handed us our keys to the hotel.

"Perfect." She handed our bags to a concierge and told us to follow him to our room. Our room was on the top floor and required our specific room key to get in through the elevator.

I followed with a smile as we rode up the elevator, preparing to ream him out when we reached the room. He didn't even consult me before pretending to be my husband. I was going to out myself and pay for the room. It wasn't like I didn't have the money. Then, Wyatt could've had his own room, and a vacation completely separate from mine.

"And here you are, the honeymoon suite for our lovers," the concierge said as the elevator entered the room. It was beautiful, for a married couple. There were sunflowers placed throughout the room, my favorite flower. Something set up by me, not my supposed-to-be husband. There was one heart-shaped bed in the room and a heart-shaped hot tub to match. The room was elegant and romantic, but it felt weird to be here with Wyatt. While the room had some reclining chairs, it didn't have a couch for either of us to sleep on, but maybe Wyatt would be comfortable with a chair.

"Thank you," I said, handing him money so he would leave faster, and I could speak to Wyatt alone.

When he did, I turned to Wyatt, who was busy taking in the beauty of the room. "Holy shit. This is nice," he said.

"You lied for me," I said, my arms crossed around my chest.

"You're welcome. You'd lose your comp if I didn't. So what, do we have to take a few pictures together? Not a big deal."

I rolled my eyes. "I can't tell my followers that I'm not married, while also creating content with my husband, Wyatt."

"What they don't know won't hurt them. They've never seen my brother, have they? You don't post pictures with him, which I think is strange, since they were so excited for your wedding."

"He didn't want to be posted, and I respected that." Before I spoke those words, I never thought about how maybe he wanted to hide me so he could appear single. If he was in my photos, millions of people, mostly women, would know who he was. He'd lose his chance to anonymously cheat. Were there other women?

"If my girlfriend had millions of followers, and was super beautiful, I'd want the world to know she's mine," he said. I didn't miss the bitter tone in his words, though I didn't know who the bitterness was meant for.

"Well, lucky for you, pretty soon the entire world will think I'm yours," I replied.

I thought about calling him Brad in videos, but it felt weird. I'd have to skip around the truth by creatively using the word we and never saying husband or Brad. I was prepared though, and thankfully we weren't live so videos could be edited.

I showed the camera my walk to the bed to showcase the beautiful flower petals, then showed Wyatt in the background unpacking into the drawers. Of course, organized Wyatt would do that. "We've made it to Florida!" I said happily, putting on a face for the world to see. "Our room is beautiful and clean, and the staff is so friendly. I'm so excited to take you guys on this journey." I hoped no one who saw the video posted to my story knew where the hotel room was, since I didn't want to be bothered by followers and potential security risks on my trip. Per my deal, I didn't have to reveal the hotel location until after my trip was over, but I did have to post content from being here. The clip was brief before it was posted, and I immediately saw the congratulations coming in.

"Did you just show my butt to the internet?"

I laughed. "Your clothed butt putting away clothes, yes. I'm sure they'll love it. If they ever know the truth, maybe you'll find your future girlfriend that way."

He shook his head and rolled his eyes. "So, what's on the itinerary for today?"

"What itinerary?" I questioned, a smirk forming on my face. "Aren't you always saying I'm unorganized?"

"You're cluttered, messy, and unorganized, that's true. When you travel, even if it's your honeymoon, you keep a detailed itinerary because you have to generate content."

He was right about the itinerary being carefully planned, but the first day wouldn't be completed. I had written where Brad and I were going to have sex all over the hotel room, and planned a dinner at his favorite restaurant. That wouldn't happen with Wyatt.

"Dinner in the hotel's restaurant, where I will record a video about the meal, and a lot of hangover sleeping," I answered, getting straight to the point. I was exhausted, hurt, and stressed. While having to pretend to be happy and in love.

"Not acceptable. This is a vacation. Honeymoon? Whatever you want to call it. It's my duty to make sure you have fun and forget about what happened at home. You know, my brother cheating on you and running off with a younger girl," he said nonchalantly with a small grin.

"The start to some good ole fun is definitely reminding me about my heartbreak."

"You're not heartbroken over Brad. You were a bad match and he wasn't good enough for you. You are heartbroken because you lost something, and that's understandable, but you also prevented the worst mistake of your life. Imagine marrying him, then finding out he's a prick."

He sure was kind, gentle, and reassuring. He shocked me by referring to his brother as a prick. I thought that no matter what, he'd have his back. Especially against me.

"I still loved him, Wyatt," I responded. It was true, but there was also truth to what he said. I was upset the wedding didn't happen, but truthfully, I was more upset about that than the fact that I'd no longer be with Brad. Wyatt's explanation made sense.

"I know. For whatever reason, you did. Now let's take your mind off of him and do something fun. The wholesome kind, not the dirty kind." he suggested.

"Do you even know what fun is?" I asked with a smirk.

"Ouch. That hurts. Of course I do, you should know that by now."

"I know you, Wyatt, which is why I ask. Fun for you is probably glaring at strangers and lifting weights at the gym," I teased.

"Are you saying those two things don't sound like a blast?" He feigned a pained expressed and grasped his heart. I rolled my eyes.

Chapter Twelve

Hannah

I was curious what Wyatt Maverick's idea of fun was. I knew he enjoyed working, going to the gym, and wearing suits, but I assumed we weren't doing any of those things together. Other than that, the only other thing I witnessed him doing was looking at me with a scowl planted on his face.

He didn't tell me what we were doing, so I changed from my flight outfit into a pair of denim shorts and a graphic t-shirt, matching his casual look.

"Why is Wyatt, the anti-vacation king, telling the travel blogger how to have a good time? That's kind of my thing, not yours."

He chuckled. "You're one of the people always telling me to take a vacation. Here I am. If you're going to force me to be on a vacation with you, I'm going to make it as fun as possible. Our job right now is to focus more on fun and less on work. Except for what you need to do for your contract."

"Forced you, huh? That's the story you're going with? Must've been so hard to convince you to go to a beautiful state, during beautiful weather, and leave the cold behind. So sorry I forced you into this trauma," I teased. He rolled his eyes.

"Our chariot has arrived," he said, opening the door for me to walk out.

We went down the hall, in the elevator, down dozens of floors, and entered the car. He gave our driver an address, refusing to tell me where we were going. I was confused about how he'd even know where to go, given that he didn't know anything about Florida. He only had roughly fifteen minutes to prepare something from when he told me we were leaving. I almost couldn't believe that Wyatt was the one who wanted to go out and do something, and I wanted to sit in the hotel and wallow.

About ten minutes later, we stopped at a small amusement park with batting cages, mini golf, and go-karting. I let out a small laugh. Brad would've never thought of doing something like this with me. Much like his brother, he was a serious person, and his fun was solely in elegant pleasures. He'd take me to a wine tasting above anything else, and if he was in a really fun mood, we might head to a museum. Not that I didn't like museums. Sometimes, I wanted to do childlike stuff like this, seeing as I didn't get these experiences as a child.

"You're prepared to get whooped in golf and go-karts?" I asked while exiting the car.

"I'm totally prepared to beat you in both and then play some arcade games," he responded.

I rolled my eyes and walked behind him to the front entrance. There was no line, so he walked up to the counter and ordered two unlimited passes for us.

"So, what's first, wife?" he asked teasingly.

"Oh God, please don't call me that again. Let's go-kart."

"And don't call me that again…unless we're in a different situation," he said, confusing me. I didn't get to question him since he turned his back towards me. I followed him to the go-kart area, and we took up two go-karts in the middle, joining another group that had just gotten in before us.

I smiled at him as it counted down to a green light, saluting him before taking off behind the people ahead of me. Most of the time during the race, he was directly next to me or inches away, but I kept ahead. I used the curve to push him inside more, and it ended up stopping him briefly, enough for me to get ahead. After the third lap, I crossed the finish line in second, and he was behind me in third.

I got out of the car slowly and set the helmet down in the seat as directed. "Look at that. I beat you!" I said, mocking and teasing him. I was shocked by my win. The only racing experience I had was on an Xbox game that Brad had. Sometimes we raced each other, other times I'd race when no one was around. A controller race didn't translate to real-world knowledge, though.

"You guys are cute. You take this very seriously," one of the girls in the race said, prompting me to laugh.

"I'm cute, he's cute, but we're not together," I responded, pointing back and forth between us.

The other group walked away, and he stood in front of me, a grin on his face. "So, you think I'm cute?"

"Uh, no, the words came out wrong," I clarified, looking down so he wouldn't know I was lying. The last thing I needed to do was give Wyatt more of an ego.

He stepped away from me and started to walk in the other direction. "Let's go mini-golf."

I nodded and walked to catch up to him. "As long as you're prepared to lose again."

I was awfully confident for someone with no experience, but I knew Wyatt didn't have any either. He grew up with a few nannies and a stay-at-home mom, but with the family and wealth he came from, fun childhood activities weren't their thing. His father was into golf, though, and tried to pass on the passion to his sons. I knew it worked with Brad, but I wasn't sure about Wyatt. The first hole was pretty straight forward, and it still took me nine tries to get it in. I was doomed to lose.

"Here, let me help," Wyatt offered. He came up behind me, wrapping his arms around me and showing me how to hold the putter. I could feel his chest against my upper back, and my breath hitched. Something about his arms around me, holding me close, felt so right yet so wrong. When he whispered his directions near my ear, he was so close that I could feel his warm breath on my neck, sending tingles down my spine. Then, he made motions with me to show me how to swing and follow through. The second hole only took me six tries.

As we went on, they got more complex, but I seemingly got better. I was still no match for Wyatt, which both shocked me and didn't at the same time. In the end, he beat me by dozens of points, but I wasn't mad.

Afterward, we played a few silly arcade games and won enough tickets for a pencil and a piece of candy.

"I'm hungry. Are you?" he asked.

"I have a reservation at Brad's favorite restaurant...let's skip it and go to McDonald's," I suggested. It felt wrong to take Wyatt there, and I wanted to keep up with the day's theme: fun, silly, childish.

The Uber that we ordered pulled up to the front curb, and we got inside the car. "You know that's super bad for your heart, right?"

"Spoken like a true Doctor. It won't kill us to eat it once," I said with certainty.

"Chicken nuggets do sound good," he agreed.

We each got six chicken nuggets and a medium fry, taking a booth in the corner and setting a tray between us. Wyatt got a cup of water while I got a Coke with no shame. I was fit, but I wasn't as much of a health nut as he was. It made sense for him since he was a doctor.

"You dip your nuggets in ketchup?" he criticized with a slight chuckle.

"Yes, of course. Ketchup is the only thing that goes with chicken nuggets."

He held up a sauce container of BBQ sauce and one of ranch. "These are the best dipping sauces, of course."

"That's an atrocity. Ranch is disgusting," I told him. I didn't mind barbecue sauce, but I only used it on specific meats, and chicken nuggets weren't one of them.

"I can't believe I came to Florida with you before knowing you hated ranch. Ouch," he said with a smile, grabbing at his heart. "It hurts. I think I'll take the first flight home tomorrow."

I rolled my eyes, focusing on eating my food. It had been months since I ate Mcdonald's, potentially even a year or more. Brad and I didn't eat out often. He didn't view my job as real, so since I "stayed home and scrolled Instagram all day," I had to cook most of the time. The more I reflected on my relationship with Brad, the more I realized it wasn't as good as I pretended. The thought of being married to a safe choice drew me to him, but he ruined that by still ending up a cheater.

How could I ever trust someone else if the person I trusted to be safe ended up a liar?

"What are you thinking about? You look sad all of a sudden," Wyatt pointed out, questioning me.

"It's so different with you. You're so different from your brother, but you come off as serious and mean," I explained. I immediately closed my mouth and regretted it, but he laughed.

"Mean? What did I do?"

"Brad told me how you told him to break up with me, and you ignored me every time we were around each other. You hated me and deemed me not good enough, just like your mother. Plus, you'd stare at me like I had murdered your cat."

"I told Brad that you're beyond out of his league, to clarify," he told me, making direct eye contact. I bit my lip, feeling the heat rise to my cheeks. "And for your information, I've never had a cat. I'm only serious and brooding because of the shit I have to see at work sometimes. It's tough. So, what's on your mind for tomorrow?" he asked, changing the subject quickly before I could respond to anything he said.

"Well, I planned this entire trip around what Brad would want and do, so I don't think the plans I made are relevant anymore. Fuck the itinerary."

"You didn't think about yourself? But that wasn't my question. What do you want to do tomorrow?"

I thought to myself for a moment before answering. "I don't know. I'm not exactly used to being asked that. It may be my honeymoon too, but this trip was to convince Brad to travel more and stop worrying so much about what your parents want. Kind of sad for his age since you clearly broke apart from what they wanted," I explained.

He laughed and nodded his head. "Understandable. But never set your wants aside for someone else's. A true partner won't let you."

I smiled. We were only on the first day of our trip, and I felt like I was learning an entire new side of Wyatt Maverick. A side I would've never guessed existed from the man that didn't keep women around for long.

Chapter Thirteen

Hannah

When we returned to the room, I was beyond ready to cozy up to some television and fall asleep. Brad and I didn't watch the same shows, so I was used to watching TV and falling asleep in the bedroom. Here, I didn't have that option. Wyatt and I had to share a room and television, and we didn't even talk about how we had to share the bed.

"If you want, I can go downstairs and grab a cot to sleep on," Wyatt offered.

"Then they'll be suspicious of why my husband is getting a cot instead of sleeping in this beautiful heart-shaped bed they gave us. We just have to suck it up," I explained.

"You don't have to make it sound like sleeping next to me is the worst thing in the world," he said lightly, with a pretend hurt voice.

"I thought I'd spend tomorrow morning waking up to a different Maverick brother," I said lightly. I took the remote from the nightstand and turned on the Food Network channel. My favorite show was on.

"Chopped, I love this show," he said before grabbing a change of clothes and walking into the bathroom, presumably putting on pajamas. I thought about how I only packed lingerie, expecting to share this honeymoon suite with my fiancé. He emerged from the bathroom moments later in a white shirt and soft plaid pants.

Brad didn't own pajamas. He said he was too warm to wear them, but I was pretty sure it was just an excuse to get away with only wearing boxers to bed, which I didn't mind. Somehow, Wyatt made pajamas look sexy. I shook my head when I noticed myself staring, but I could tell by his chuckle that he already caught me.

"You can't go to bed in that," Wyatt noted, looking at me up and down.

"About that…"

He laughed. "You didn't bring normal pajamas, did you?" he questioned with a cocked eyebrow and a tilted head.

"No, I did not," I said honestly.

He rummaged through his drawer before throwing a pair of basketball shorts and yet another white shirt at me. "You sure are a fan of plain white shirts," I noted.

I watched as he jumped in the bed and got comfortable, laying on his side and propping himself up with his elbow so he could watch the show. Either I'd have to stare awkwardly at him or lay in front of him to watch television and hope we didn't get close enough to spoon. Thankfully, the bed was large enough for four people.

"Thanks for today," I told him while facing the television, hiding the smile on my face.

It felt nice to eat somewhere familiar instead of somewhere with dishes I had never heard of and wine that cost more than my car payment.

"So, have you decided what you want to do tomorrow?" he questioned.

"Well, I was thinking of a naked couples massage, but you took that off the table. How about we start in the spa, and then we can think about dinner?" I joked about the naked massage. Kind of. A couples massage was included in the package I got from the hotel, but I hadn't booked one.

"And when will we swim with dolphins? This is Florida."

"That's in five days. I made the reservations earlier," I answered.

"Wait, we're actually swimming with dolphins?"

"Yes, of course. It's Florida."

"Who the hell even honeymoons in Florida? Why not go somewhere out of the country?"

I bit my lip. He couldn't have known how much that comment would hurt me. "Our first vacation together was to Disney World. We came here every year, and it seemed like the place we wanted to celebrate our new marriage."

"Remind me to punch him in the face when we return," he said.

"I think I already got that covered," I reminded him. I still felt a tinge of pain in my fist where my knuckles clashed with his face, but I was proud of the pain. Thinking about what he did to me was worse. Remembering our lives over the past five years was a pain unlike anything I had ever felt. And Nicole's betrayal stung.

I knew Wyatt wasn't fond of me. The Wyatt on this trip was not the same Wyatt back home who would glare at me with thin lips when I was around and remind me how annoying my presence was when I was at their house. He was nice to me because he felt terrible, but I wondered if our dynamic would change when we returned home - until I remembered he wouldn't be in my life anymore.

"I love my brother, but he can be an idiot. He deserved that. I can't believe he cheated on you and got someone else pregnant. Can you imagine those two idiots raising a baby together?" he said with a chuckle in an attempt to lighten the mood.

"When I think about it, I puke. I didn't say this, but thanks for coming with me, Wyatt. I'm having fun, minus the crying in the shower," I admitted.

"It's my job to make you cry as little as possible. Tomorrow is a new day to try. Let's get some sleep," he suggested. I grabbed the remote and turned off the television before setting the remote down on the nightstand and laying as close to the edge as possible to make sure our bodies weren't near each other as we slept.

Chapter Fourteen

Hannah

Despite being with Brad for five years, I refused to let him sleep close to me. We shared a bedroom in our condo and had a king-size bed. We slept several feet apart. If he started to cuddle me, a sleepy, angry version of me would grumble until he left me alone. I thought it was just that I didn't like to touch in my sleep, but when I woke up next to Wyatt, our bodies were touching, and I wasn't complaining. Despite feeling his body against my back and arm around my waist, I hadn't moved yet. I didn't know when we ended up in this position, but it made my chest rise and fall quickly.

Once the realization hit and I felt wrong for enjoying it, I leaped out of bed quickly, standing away from him and staring at the bed as I tried to process what I felt. Excitement to be briefly touched by a man who wasn't Brad. Even though I wasn't excited to touch Brad.

Wyatt slowly opened his eyes as I stood on the opposite side of the room.

"Are you watching me sleep?" he questioned with his bed hair and a small smirk as he lay on his side and rested his cheek in his palm.

"Don't flatter yourself. I just woke up and jumped out of bed so fast to get away from you," I teased, making light of an awkward situation that he wasn't aware even happened.

"I was promised a spa day today. When do I get a nice massage?" he winked. I wouldn't give him the satisfaction of knowing that his wink, combined with his messy morning look, made my stomach flip.

"Well, it's nine, and we're supposed to be down there at ten. So we have time to shower, and I'll be taking the first shower," I said, looking around for my bag to grab my bathroom stuff and a change of clothes.

He was already at the bathroom door before I could finish grabbing my stuff. "Not if I get in there first," he said before shutting the door and locking it.

"You're a pain in my ass, Wyatt Maverick," I said while standing directly outside the door so he could hear me shout.

I expected him to take a short shower like he did before the flight, but he didn't come out for fifteen minutes. When I heard the water stop, I shouted into the door again, "You went so fast you don't even have a change of clothes or shower products."

Before I stepped away, he opened the door, standing on the other side with a towel wrapped around his waist. "I don't need to change until I'm done, and I use the hotel shampoo, conditioner, and soap. What else do I need?"

I blinked a few times while assessing if this was my life. I was on my honeymoon with my fiancé's brother, who was half-naked with only a towel on. Only one part of him was left up to my imagination. "You like to be half-naked, don't you?"

"No one has ever complained before, but I forgot I'm with the only woman not attracted to me," he responded. I rolled my eyes for several reasons. But I wasn't about to tell him I was attracted to him, so I didn't want to see him in a towel.

I knew it didn't make sense. If he was anyone else, I would've made a move in an attempt to get Brad off my mind.

"You don't have your own shampoo, conditioner, or soap you prefer?" I asked, grabbing the shower caddy I prepared with all the brands I liked, including my favorite razor and luxury loofah I received once in a brand deal.

"I use three-in-one back home. You have way too many different things, you know?" he said, his eyes glaring at the products in the basket in my hand.

"It's called good hygiene, dickbag." I said before locking myself in the bathroom, turning on the water before he could get in another word.

"For being a woman in her twenties, your insults sound like they came from a twelve-year-old on Call Of Duty," Wyatt said from the other side of the door. I laughed, but pretended that I couldn't hear him through the water. Call Of Duty was one of the games we used to play. It served as a social experiment. Wyatt would be playing and win, then he'd give me the mic, and I'd get torn to shreds because they thought a girl was beating them. Then, Wyatt would play and use the mic, and they'd treat him like a God.

When I left the bathroom twenty minutes later, Wyatt was on the phone. How he spoke to someone reminded me of the more serious, business-oriented Wyatt I knew from home. I should've expected he couldn't go a week without doing some work.

"I got the results back, and I'll call her normal medication into her regular pharmacy. Just call me if you need anything. My phone is on even if I'm out of town," he offered the person on the other end before hanging up. "I have to call the pharmacy before we go," he told me.

"You're not supposed to be doing work. It's vacation, you said so," I pointed out.

"You're doing work," he responded. He had a point.

"My work is a video or two a day, which takes a few minutes," I responded.

"If you ignore the time, you bring out your phone and scroll online, or start taking notes for your blog, sick children can't wait, unlike your work," he said with a monotone before walking to the desk and sitting down, making the call to the pharmacy.

The mean Wyatt from home, who didn't know how he acted, sure was making a return. He had never made a jab at my career like that, and it was unlike him.

"I'll be outside whenever you're ready." He waved me off with his hand, and I exited the hotel room.

Chapter Fifteen

Hannah

Wyatt joined me in the hall five minutes later, and we started quietly walking toward the spa. He donned a bright blue Hawaiian shirt with pink flowers, khaki shorts, and sandals. The smile on his face told me that the mood from before was gone, and the happy vacation side of Wyatt was back.

I rolled my eyes when I looked at him, unaware that he caught my judging glance.

"You dig it, right?" he asked with a grin. "I brought it to your wedding as a joke when I was sitting by the pool enjoying my vacation."

"You look like a bright flower shop threw up on you."

"Listen, I'm sorry about a few minutes ago, okay? It was one of my longtime patients, she's sick, and it's scary for me. I care about her. I care about all my patients."

We exited the elevator at the lobby level, which was where most of the amenities were located. "I'm sorry about your patient," I said.

I walked ahead to arrive at the spa desk first to check us in.

"Hi, excuse me, I have two massages set up under the name Maverick," I said, hoping the hint of pain didn't come out in my voice. I was expected to be Mrs. Maverick when I booked the spa last week.

"Ah, yes, the couples massage class," she said with a bright smile.

My eyes widened. "That's definitely not what I booked,"

"What is a couples massage class?" Wyatt questioned from behind me.

"It's complimentary from the hotel for the honeymoon package, Mrs. Maverick. You'll have a private, one-on-one session with a massage therapist who will teach you how to give each other a lovely massage. Dim lighting, perfect environment, and aromatherapy for relaxation."

"I think I'll just, uh, take my own room," Wyatt said. Even the idea of touching me repulsed him. Not that I wanted to touch him, either. It was like he woke up and realized how much he didn't like my presence.

"Yeah, what he said," I agreed. The women briefly looked frightened by our need to be separated.

"Getting this class is something couples would kill you for," she said with a serious face. It took all my energy not to laugh.

"Well, here we are," Wyatt said with a chuckle, "ready for the taking."

"We'll take it, thank you. That's really thoughtful," I said, catching Wyatt's wide eyes as he looked back at me.

"Yes, I guess we will. Thank you very much."

When they were ready for us, we went into separate rooms to change into our own robes. They taught by showing. Lucky me. I kept on my underwear and tightly wrapped the robe around myself, making sure no areas were exposed as I walked into the room.

"Welcome, happy couple. Congratulations on your marriage!" The woman instructor said to us once I arrived in the room. I could see on Wyatt's face that he was just as nervous as me.

"Who would like to learn first?" she asked.

I raised my hand fast to avoid having his hands on me first. Either way, it would be an awkward and intimate moment. I knew he'd hate it and felt somewhat bad for putting us in this position.

Wyatt smirked before he shrugged his shoulders. "Guess I'll receive first."

"Bet you're used to saying that," I teased. I watched Wyatt's face contour to hold back laughter.

"Just remove your robe and lay face down on the table," she instructed.

He followed her directions, and she put a towel over the parts of him already covered by his boxers. Wyatt, the serious doctor with money to blow, wore lavish silk boxers. A different contrast from the dozens of cotton plaid ones that graced all corners of our floors at home. Rather, my former home. I'd have to deal with that reality next week.

"Now, we're focused on a nice, sensual, and intimate massage you can do at home. I'll have you use some jojoba oil before we start and rub it well into your hands. The most important thing to remember is not to go for the bones. Massaging is about the muscles," she instructed while squirting a bit of oil into my hands.

"Start here, and just knead your palms into him. Not too harsh," she directed, pointing to his shoulders. I took a deep breath before pushing my slick palms into his shoulders, trying not to press too rough. His shoulders - and his entire body - were full of muscles.

"It smells like your perfume in here," Wyatt said, and I couldn't tell if he was disgusted or not. It took me a minute to process that he knew what I smelled like. Lavender.

"That's the lavender candles we have to help you relax and take your mind off stressful things, so you can be in the moment."

I blushed. "It's my favorite scent."

"Mine too," Wyatt mumbled into his face pillow before clearing his throat like he didn't mean to say that.

"Now, slowly work your hands down his back and to his lower back, kneading along the sides."

I followed the instructions and paused my hands in the middle of his back. Going to his lower back felt way more intimate than what we were doing. She started to stare at me, and I moved my hands lower, rubbing until my hands were in the small of his back. Wyatt emitted a small groan as I pushed on a rough muscle he had. That sound forced me to remove my hands from his back. I was sure he felt as awkward as I did.

"Now onto the legs," she said with a grin.

Five minutes later, it was my turn. There was a separate bed for me. Wyatt turned around when she instructed me to de-robe, and she put the towel over me. If she thought it was weird that my husband wasn't looking at me while I was half-naked, she didn't say anything.

"Her shoulders look really tense. Let's start there," she said.

I was tense. My fiancé's brother had his hands on my body. He disliked me, but he was here massaging me. In Florida. On a honeymoon. I certainly didn't see this coming a few days ago.

I had never seen a side of Wyatt that wasn't serious, except for how he wasn't serious about relationships. Maybe the massage meant nothing to him because a woman's body was nothing but a normal thing for him to touch. He was good at it; he knew all the right places to touch.

He made his way down until he was rubbing my calf, his slick hands slowly slipping up my leg. He stopped at my upper thigh, kneading his palm into the muscle around my leg in a way that felt so good that I needed to bite my lip to hold back from making any unwanted sounds that would make the day even more awkward.

"Now, most people don't go for it, but if you wish, I can teach you how to rub her feet just right," the instructor offered.

To my surprise, Wyatt said yes. I sat partially up and looked back at him for a moment with a cocked eyebrow, and he had a grin on his face like he was enjoying torturing me. He'd torment me over this for years to come. I just knew it.

It seemed like magic once she showed him all the right places to press into. Brad hated feet and would never dare go near them, even when I begged after being on my feet for days on end, walking through cities and exploring.

"Your feet are so…delicate," he said.

"You make that sound like an insult," I pointed out. He chuckled.

"You know," I said, pulling my feet away from his grasp, "we have so much to do today, but thank you for the lesson. You've been great."

"Yeah, I can't wait to rub my wife's feet after a long day when we're home," Wyatt said with a heartbreaking smirk.

Chapter Sixteen

Wyatt

The minute she left the hotel room after I sent her away, I felt like an ass. I couldn't even vacation properly, but hopefully, I'd get it right by the time I was on my real honeymoon. I hoped that my future honeymoon also involved Hannah and that time, we'd put work away for real. I'd take her wherever she wanted, unlike Brad. I also wouldn't let her foot the bill for the entire wedding. As much as Brad liked traditional gender roles, he sure did mooch off her money, despite him having millions.

I hope that my change in attitude when I left the room showed her I was sorry. I couldn't exactly give up work entirely, but I wanted to give a real vacation a try and be the kind of guy that can have fun without a schedule. I hoped I was conveying that message because Hannah knew me well, even if she thought she didn't. She knew my habits and attitude. She knew my excitement for organization, schedules, and work. But she needed to know I could be a good guy with time for her.

I saw the way her face shifted when I tried to ask for my own massage room. She was trying to hide it, but she was hurt. I wasn't rejecting her like she thought; I was scared to have her touch me. Scared she'd realize how much I actually wanted her. Afraid to be vulnerable.

Whenever her hands pressed into my body, I had to work extra hard to control my body's reaction. Her touch was electrifying, and I felt it in my bones. I had been waiting years for a moment that I thought would never happen.

The room smelled like her lavender perfume, which drove my senses crazy. The room was designed to be relaxing, but I could hardly relax. I had to think about things that would control the urge.

Remember that time your hamster died? Remember your grandma baking you cookies? Those thoughts helped, for now.

But when it was my turn, and I heard her release a noise that would drive me wild if we were alone, I almost lost it. A semi started to form in my pants, but the instructor's voice made it disappear, thankfully. I didn't want Hannah to be scared to be around me or think I was a pervert.

I was surprisingly thankful when the instructor taught me how to massage her feet thoroughly. I was being honest when I said I'd massage my wife's feet one day because she deserved that treatment from a man. She just didn't know that I was hoping it was her.

Chapter Seventeen

Hannah

"T he foot rubbing thing was a nice touch there, making yourself seem like the perfect husband to me," I told him as we walked to our next spa appointment: pedicures. I was happy that Wyatt agreed to participate with me. I hated comparing him to his brother constantly. Still, spending time conversing with Wyatt showed me how much I had overlooked about Brad, including that Brad would never go into a nail salon with me for my monthly appointments.

"It wasn't a lie, though. When my future wife asks for a foot rub, I'll give her one. I'd want her to know she's loved, valued, and appreciated, and I'd show that in any way I could." Wyatt's response sent a funny feeling to my core, one I hadn't felt in a while. Probably since I first met Brad, before things got complicated.

"What an interesting statement from a man I once saw break up with a girl he saw twice with a muffin basket. Then immediately bring home another girl."

Wyatt chuckled, his hand ruffling the hair on the back of his head. "You and Brad moved out over a year ago, Hannah. Things change. People change. Or maybe I had a reason for how I acted in the past, and you judged me without trying to figure it out because it was easier for you to be disgusted by me."

I wondered what could happen to a man to make him care so little about relationships and connections, but I felt terrible because he was right. I judged him for years without having honest conversations with him. I suppose you couldn't break up with someone you were never even officially dating.

"I'm sorry," was all I could say. "And if you ever want to talk about what made you act that way back then, I'll be here. For now, I'll try to look at you in a new light," I offered.

"Maybe one day I'll be ready," he said softly.

When we arrived at the nail area of the hotel's giant spa, a woman was there to greet us. She showed me the nail polish and said I could pick one out for my toenails if I wanted.

"Excuse me," Wyatt said as she started to walk away.

She stopped walking and turned around with a smile on her face. "Yes, sir?"

"I wasn't offered a color. Am I allowed to pick one? What if I want pink toenails?"

I held back a laugh. It didn't seem like Wyatt to want to paint his toes, but it wasn't like I ever looked at his feet.

"Of course."

Wyatt went to the spinning cart next to mine and picked up a neon pink color, showing it to me. "What about this?" he asked.

"Sure, if that's what you want," I said through gritted teeth, which made Wyatt laugh.

"I think I'll stick with this," he said, holding a bottle of black nail polish.

"And I'll match my nails that I had done for the wedding," I said, waving a silver glitter polish in the air.

"Congrats on the marriage, folks. We're ready for you, come on back," the receptionist said when she walked back up to us. Wyatt and I both cleared out throats to hold back a laugh when she congratulated us.

We got up and followed her back, where she led us to two recliners next to each other and handed out pedicure menus.

"No need," Wyatt said, "we'll each take the deluxe with the avocado mask included."

"Someone's experienced," I remarked.

"It should be way more normal for men to get their feet and hands taken care of. Pedicures and manicures are a monthly thing for me," he replied, quieting me. I agreed with him. It was a point I made to Brad far too often, but it never changed his mind.

One day, a girl would be lucky to end up with him.

Two women walked up a minute later and started the tubs at our feet. They introduced themselves as our pedicurists. As they started working on our feet, someone else threw on an avocado mud mask, which stiffened my face.

"Would you like complimentary wine?" she asked, flashing a bottle of Caymus Cabernet Sauvignon.

"Yes," Wyatt and I answered simultaneously, laughing.

"That mask makes you look like an alien," I said when we made eye contact.

"Then I guess that makes you look like one, too, since we have the same mask on after all."

"Wow, this is very good," I remarked, taking a sip of the wine. "And I've been wine tasting through Italy, so I think I know my wine well."

"That was the most pretentious thing I've heard you say. You're turning into influencer Hannah again, not that I dislike her, but you don't need to be that person around me," Wyatt said. I didn't realize what he was even talking about. I was Hannah the influencer. There aren't two sides to me.

"That's because I am one, Wyatt. I did a three-week Italy trip to taste hundreds of wines across the country. And the blogs and videos got millions of hits and inspired people to send me photos of their travels to Italy. I even rated all the wines as I went."

Wyatt rolled his eyes. "I've known you since before you reached one hundred thousand followers, Hannah. You may be the Hannah who goes on luxurious vacations for work and blogs about it for millions of people. Still, you're the same Hannah I saw wake up with messy hair, a drooling face, and in the same pajamas worn by every other regular person. Don't forget that. I saw you during that time."

"I was not drooling." I didn't even know I had become a pretentious-sounding person just because of my job and the persona I had to keep up for views and attention. "And speaking of influencing," I said, grabbing my phone from my bag sitting next to me. "Hey, guys! We're on day two of our honeymoon," I briefly flashed the camera to Wyatt, "and getting pedicures done. The spa at this hotel is uh-mazing, and I can't wait for you guys to visit one day. I can't wait to reveal the name next week." I turned off the video and slid my phone back into my pocket. "Work done for the day already."

"It's amazing how you can get your work done in thirty seconds and call it a day," he noted. "Maybe I should change careers."

I laughed. "Yeah, right, Wyatt Maverick taking a break from work and experiencing life. He hasn't done that since before college."

"What do you think I'm doing right now?" he said, and it was a fair question. But I knew Wyatt, and I knew he hadn't taken a vacation since before he entered medical school. He was only here because he took time off to watch his brother get married...and that failed. He missed our engagement party because he had an office emergency at eight in the evening.

"I think you're enjoying your first trip in like a decade by hijacking my honeymoon," I said. I stopped myself from saying anything else when I remembered we weren't alone, and he was my faux husband. He wouldn't hijack a honeymoon he was on.

"It's not that bad, is it? I can take a vacation whenever, since I own the practice," he explained.

"Except you won't delegate the work and hire someone else. Someone to cover time off, to come in after hours when people need help, and you want to do normal things."

"Working non-stop is normal in this country," he joked, prompting yet another eye roll. He wasn't wrong, though.

"I'd slap you in the shoulder again, but I'd hate to hurt you," I said with a smile.

"You mean you want to keep your other hand free from harm? I get it. It's not like your hit could hurt."

"Tell that to your brother's face and my fist," I said. I was caught off guard when he took my hand and examined it. My knuckles had changed colors as they became bruised. They were still a little sore, and I winced as he applied pressure. Something in his careful attention made the moment so intimate. I try to make light of the situation by cracking a joke. "I bet Brad's face matches the color of my knuckles."

"I can FaceTime him right now if you'd like. It's okay. You can tell me you miss my brother," he said with a smirk, and I knew he was teasing me. The pedicurists gave each other looks that clearly conveyed their confusion about our conversation. Why would my husband insist I miss his brother?

My feet were taken out of the tub and wrapped in a warm towel; by now, my wine glass was almost empty.

"You should probably slow down on the wine since we know how you get when you drink too much."

"No. You know how I get. You won't tell me the things I said still," I pointed out. He was right, though, considering I had a massive headache the next morning and felt sluggish the entire day. But it was a vacation, and I didn't care. In under a week, I'd have to return to a reality I didn't want to face. While looking him in the eye, I chugged the rest of the wine.

My pedicurist, who had started to work on my toenails, let out an audible giggle.

Chapter Eighteen

Hannah

Wyatt invited me to lunch with him after we left the hotel spa. I wanted to say yes, but I wanted to use the time to call Priya while he was out of the room since it was my first time alone since I saw her last. Wyatt agreed to bring me food, and when I asked him where he was eating so I could give him an order, he said he'd surprise me. He walked out of the hotel so fast that I couldn't stop him.

Priya squealed on the other line when she picked up my call. "Tell me everything," she demanded.

"Relax, Priya. We've been here a few days. Not much has happened, obviously," I reminded her.

"And in less than a day, your relationship fell apart, and you were on a plane with your fiancé's brother, may I remind you?" she said. She meant no harm, but her words stung. One thing I appreciated about Priya was her brutal honesty. She had no filter and wasn't afraid to speak her mind, which could also get her in trouble.

"Thanks for the reminder, babe. Have you...have you seen him?" I asked. I was unsure if I was going to mention anything. Normally, I wouldn't expect anyone to see either of them, but she was Nicole's cousin and, therefore, much more likely to see them than my other friends. "Oh, and what are people saying?" I wasn't sure I wanted to know.

Priya remained silent for a few moments. I knew she didn't have anything good to say. "Yeah, I did. He came begging to know your location and saying he was sorry. Nicole is pissed. He started ignoring her. And are you sure you want to know what people are saying?"

"You didn't tell him, did you? And yes, of course I do."

I started to panic. Clearly, no one had nice things to say about what happened, yet no one reached out to me. Millions of followers, and I couldn't even get my closest friends to ask me if I was okay when they witnessed me discovering my fiancé cheating.

"Hell no, I wouldn't betray you like that. Brad can eat a bag of dicks for all I care." Priya sighed, seemingly conflicted on if she wanted to tell me the information I asked for. Well, okay, you asked for it. Olivia and Isabella said you were cheating with his brother the entire time, Lillian said you were a whore, and Megan said you never deserved Brad anyways because you put your career before his needs." Priya's honesty struck again.

A whore? It was a weird comment from the girl who preaches feminism and loving yourself to half a million people. But when all your friends embellish their lives for likes and views, you can't be surprised when those people show themselves as fake.

"You've known me my whole life, Priya. Do you think I'm pretentious?" I asked, reminded of Wyatt's comment earlier. Priya was one of the few friends who met me before I was Hannah, the travel blogger. She knew me when I was Hannah, the elementary school child, Hannah, the teen with braces, and Hannah, the girl who lost her virginity in college.

"Well, I, uh, I mean, you're different than before. I wouldn't quite say pretentious. The Hannah I knew growing up would've never ditched her friends to take a trip across the globe, use her following to say bad things about a business, or date a guy so obnoxiously boring just because she needed to put out the perfect image. You care so much about what others think that sometimes you're fake just to help the narrative. But, that same Hannah would've never punched her cheating scumbag fiancé and run off with his brother. I'm proud of that part. Now spill the details."

If Priya brought my bad habits to light, then I was truly not as good as I thought. Wyatt was right about me. When I was with Brad earlier in our relationship and stayed with them, I'd wake up and be completely honest about how I looked. It was one thing that brought attention to my channel early on. Now, I wouldn't dare be on camera if I wasn't wearing makeup and didn't brush my hair and change into my pink silk pajamas that were just for show.

No wonder I had no close friends who would check up on me.

"So far, we went go-karting, got pedicures, and had to touch each other half-naked."

"Please elaborate on the half-naked thing. Why didn't you start the conversation with that?"

I laughed. "It was a couples massage class. We learned how to massage each other. But my most intimate part wasn't when his hand grazed my thigh. It was when he rubbed my feet. I've never let anyone touch my feet."

"You hate feet. Touching them, others touching yours. That's a big step. I bet you'll be pregnant tomorrow." How she could tell a joke without laughing or cracking a smile made her jokes so much more enjoyable. Sometimes, people couldn't tell when she was joking.

"Wyatt and Hannah sitting in a tree," Priya started to sing.

"Don't you dare finish that," I warned. "We haven't kissed, and we're not going to. This is nothing. He's going to go back to hating me when we return, and everything will be normal," I reminded her.

"Remember that time that you went over, and he scowled at you, then left the apartment? So strange that the same man who did that is the same man who agreed to go on your honeymoon with you."

"I think he pities me. I'm having fun, but I can't wait for this to end. I didn't even mention the worst part. Wyatt is pretending to be Brad, my husband. To the hotel and to my followers," I told her.

"This conversation gets more interesting by the minute. I'm never going to let anyone call you basic ever again. How the hell did this even happen?" she asked.

"Who calls me basic?"

"Who doesn't? You look like every blonde on Pinterest, grab Starbucks every morning, and for crying out loud, you got a pair of Ugg boots for Christmas. I'm not even sure those have been in since two thousand and ten." Being on the phone instead of in person seemed to give Priya a boldness she didn't have before since she chose to speak her mind now about things she clearly held onto for a while.

"Point taken. When we checked in, I was reminded that I was being comped the hotel room and had a contract. It wasn't like I needed the comp, I could've admitted the truth and just paid, but I did have a contract. When Wyatt offered to pretend, I...didn't stop him. I don't know," I admitted. Truthfully, I could've stopped this from happening before it started. I could've even stopped the trip, but some of me didn't want to. Though I traveled a lot, I was hardly spontaneous unless I got a last-minute deal. Even then, I'd still plan meticulously. My trip, my postings, and everything about my travel was more work than play, but this felt more spontaneous, and I couldn't pass up the opportunity.

"Are you guys sharing a room then?" she pried.

"Worse, we're sharing a bed," I informed her.

Her silence said more than words could. "Scandalous," she finally mustered. "Do you guys cuddle each other to sleep?"

I laughed. "God, no. I try to stay as far away as possible. It actually wasn't my first time waking up next to him. Before we left, I woke up next to him. I had a raging hangover, but he swears we didn't do anything that night, and I believe him."

"Wyatt may be an ass to you, but he's definitely a gentleman."

"I'm sure all the girls he used for a one-night stand agree," I said harshly. I told Wyatt I'd try to think of him in a different light. He was single, and he was allowed to sleep around with whomever he wanted.

"You act like women can't use men for sex or like they weren't willing participants. I'm sure they have an agreement," she made a good argument.

"You're right," I agreed. Before she could say another word, I heard the door being opened. "Got to go," I told her, quickly hanging up the phone.

"You in here talking to yourself?" Wyatt teased as he set the food down on the hotel's desk table.

"Just talking to Priya. Catching up briefly on things. What did you bring?" I asked.

"Something simple. Something we used to order every Friday," he said with a smile.

On Fridays, Brad and I would dedicate ourselves to playing video games or watching a movie, and Wyatt was always there, though he'd stay quiet in my presence and only play against Brad.

"Double pepperoni pizza," I said. I answered correctly, and he pulled a box out of the bag, handing me my New York-style pizza slice. It was my favorite kind of pizza. Wyatt kept surprising me on our trip. "Thanks, Wyatt. You know me much more than I ever gave you credit for."

"I may not have talked much to you before, but that doesn't mean I wasn't paying attention," he said.

I started eating my pizza slice to hide that I didn't know how to respond.

Chapter Nineteen

Wyatt

I didn't necessarily have a game plan when I left the room. Had Hannah agreed to go with me, I would have let her choose where she wanted to eat. When I asked her what she wanted, she told me to surprise her. I hadn't lived with her for years, so I wasn't sure if her tastes were the same, but I hoped they were.

Hannah loved the New York-style pizza we shared every Friday. We'd play video games and eat pizza with Brad, our one tradition since we were all available those nights. I had only played with him, though, and I bet she thought I was sexist about women gamers. In reality, I didn't want to play against her because her playing Call Of Duty with us was super fucking hot. Her killing me repeatedly would only make my heart grow fonder, and I didn't need that.

Near the hotel was a New York-style pizza shop, and I got lucky. I had only wandered a few buildings down when I saw it. There were a dozen pizza toppings for slices, and my eyes settled on the double pepperoni I knew she loved. That girl could eat pepperoni straight from the package, that's how much she loved it.

I picked up a few slices to bring them back to Hannah.

As I was walking, my phone started to ring. Since I was a doctor, I never ignored it. But it was Brad, and I had to think for a moment before deciding to answer the phone. Had he figured out I actually went with her? He probably thought I wouldn't do it. Or he knew me well, and he knew I would. I might have acted like I was going to say no, but I never would have. She had a hold on me.

"Yes, brother?" I greeted.

"Where is she, Wyatt? She hasn't texted me back. She hasn't come back to the apartment." I couldn't help but chuckle.

"Let's say I know where she is. Why are you texting her and trying to talk to her when you just cheated on her? You embarrassed her on her wedding day, jackass."

"It took me losing her to realize I wanted her. I think I have a chance, man. I love her," he pleaded. I was utterly baffled by his admission. I refused to believe thar my brother, who graduated in accounting with honors, was such an idiot. He didn't lack book smarts, but he certainly lacked common sense.

"If she wanted to talk to you, I'm sure she would. She's a big girl, Brad. She can make her own choices. And one of those choices just happened to lead her to me. So leave her alone. You're my brother, but you're being an idiot."

"You can't keep me from her just because you want her all to yourself."

I scuffed. "I'm not keeping her anything. It's no secret I want her, but I haven't told her to not contact you. I've just been having fun with her."

I could almost hear his anger through the phone as I mentioned having fun with her. Of course, he took that the wrong way.

"Don't touch her. She's not yours."

"She's not anyone's, Brad. She's a fucking person."

I hung up on him, angrily shoved my phone in my pocket, and headed back into the hotel. I flashed the front desk people a smile on my way up, playing my role as a doting newlywed husband. I'd happily accept the position, if it were offered.

When I got to our room and paused to grab my key, I heard her talking, and it clearly wasn't to herself.

"You act like women can't use men for sex or like they weren't willing participants. I'm sure they have an agreement," Priya's voice said.

I knew she was referring to me. I thought about listening to the rest, but I knew she probably said everything good about me when I first left. I smirked to myself. In some way, she was thinking about me sexually. I liked the thought. Instead of waiting to see what she'd say next, I opened the door, brought her lunch, and told her about the dinner reservations I made for tonight.

Chapter Twenty

Hannah

He told me he was taking me to an Italian restaurant but refused to name the place. He said that we had reservations that would put him in a tux and me in a dress, and thankfully, I brought a few cute ones. I barricaded myself in the bathroom to get ready. I curled my hair to perfection once I was dry from the shower. For makeup, I went light, with a bit of glitter on my eyelid and a little blush on my cheeks. I threw on a deep red lipstick that I knew would last through eating and drinking.

He was already ready and waiting for me so we could get picked up. He gave me a deadline of 5:30, and I was fifteen minutes away from that deadline, with nothing left but to pick the perfect dress. I went with a red, silk, tight-fitting dress with spaghetti straps and a small thigh slit on the left side. I chose the dress due to the elegant-looking drape collar on top. My other dress option was cute, but it was a pink cotton summer dress, and I was dressing up tonight.

I left the bathroom. Wyatt, dressed in his suit and tie, greeted me on the other side of the door. . I almost walked into him, that's how close to the door he was. Despite being fully covered head-to-toe, his body still managed to look hot. The suit was well-fitted to accentuate his muscular build. My lips parted as I took him in, and I could tell he noticed when he smirked at me.

"Ready to go?" he questioned. I nodded my head.

He walked out of the hotel room first, and I followed behind him. Once outside, I was shocked when he took us to a black Aston Martin with a driver standing outside the door.

"Good evening, Mr. and Mrs. Maverick," he greeted, smiling at Wyatt. I shifted uncomfortably, waiting for Wyatt to correct him, figuring he didn't want to pretend to be my husband when he didn't need to be.

"Good evening to you too, Tom." Did he know the man? "Hannah, this is our hired driver for the evening. I asked the hotel what I could do to make tonight a special night, and they suggested the driving service and restaurant," he explained.

The way he thought everything out was sweet. I wasn't used to that. I wasn't used to being the one being taken care of. A tear dripped down my face before I realized it, but Wyatt saw it and frowned.

"What's wrong?" he asked, sitting in the back of the car with me after Tom opened our door.

"I just can't believe you'd go through these lengths for me. The girl that was going to marry your brother. You don't even like me."

"Don't ever say I don't like you, Hannah. One day soon, you'll realize that's not true."

I wanted to tell him what I heard him say, or remind him of how he looked at me whenever I was around. Instead, I didn't. I stayed silent during our ride, but he placed his hand over mine, and I felt his eyes on me as I stared out the window.

Once we arrived at our destination, Tom opened the door for us and let us outside. He told us he'd return when we called but would stay parked nearby. From the moment we entered the restaurant, I could tell this place would have Wyatt spending a lot. I felt a pang of guilt in my chest since I wasn't used to being paid for, but he told me he was going to. I wasn't allowed to bring any form of payment.

"This place seems...familiar," I said, looking around at the bright gold decorations adorning the walls and the red accents. It was beautiful.

"That's because you saw it on a show once and said you wanted to visit. You thought I was studying, but I wasn't. I just didn't want you to know that I enjoyed the same shows as you." He frowned at the memory. I didn't get a chance to respond because our waiter showed up. Wyatt continued to shock me every few hours.

"What will you have to drink?" our waiter asked Wyatt.

"Bring us your best bottle of red wine," he demanded before looking at me. "Do you like red wine?" he questioned.

"I prefer white," I answered.

"Make that white wine." My eyes widened in surprise at the change. Red was his favorite, but he was ordering mine. A bottle that would cost hundreds of dollars. The waiter ran off and brought back a bottle, pouring us some and leaving it on the table. He gave us a few more minutes to order. I ordered some extremely fancy ravioli, and Wyatt ordered a dish that I believed was Octopus, but I wasn't going to ask to find out.

"How's the wine?" he asked with a smile as I took my first sip. I had the brand before and knew it was good.

"Expensive," I responded with a smirk, batting my eyelashes at him. Something about wine made me flirtatious, even if my mind was trying to scream that he was my ex-fiance's brother. There was some sort of bro or family code against this, surely.

"Worth every penny," he responded. I felt he wasn't talking about the wine for some reason.

The food looked incredible when it came out. It must have to Wyatt, too, because he finished his dish well before I did.

"So, what are you thinking about doing tomorrow?" he questioned.

"Well, you haven't had any input yet. What do you want to do?"

"It's your honeymoon. I'm just tagging along," he responded with a wink. His wink always caused butterflies in my stomach and a flutter of my heart.

"Well, I did buy two tickets to a dinner cruise on a lake. Might as well not let them go to waste. It's supposed to have fantastic views. Before that, though, we could go to the pool on the roof. They have an infinity pool, with a bar *in* the pool," I proposed the idea. Wyatt wasn't going to say no to anything I said, but I wanted him to have fun, too.

"Anything you want to do, just let me know. It's your vacation too, and you don't get many of those," I told him in a whisper, feeling bad for calling attention to something he already knew about himself.

"Spending a day with you in a bikini sounds perfect to me," he said. He cleared his throat after, and a rosy color took over his cheeks. The way he responded to how he complimented me made me smile to myself. I didn't know Wyatt had it in him to be nervous. Not knowing how to respond to that, I looked to change the subject.

"We should make a day of it. Rent a poolside cabana and eat lunch there. I heard their lunch food in the upstairs restaurant is a seafood menu. I remember you have a taste for the finer things in seafood, and they have fresh crab and lobster. Even though I tend to stick to frozen fish."

The waiter took our plates away, then returned with our bill, handing it to Wyatt. He said he was paying for it, so I knew it was happening, but letting someone else pay for my meal made my skin itch. I had the urge to jump over the table and take it for myself.

"That sounds like a fun time." Wyatt looked at the bill without flinching before turning to me. "Do you want dessert?"

I blinked a few times. Even if I did, I wouldn't tell him because I didn't want him to spend more money on me.

"For fuck's sake, Hannah, spend my money. Stop worrying about it," he said in a gentle tone, despite his words seeming harsh. It was lighthearted. When the waiter returned, he ordered tiramisu, sorbet, and a slice of chocolate cake with more things listed on it than I expected. And it was more expensive than buying an entire cake at a grocery store.

"Really, you don't have to do that, Wyatt. Why three?"

"I want you to have whatever you want and feel guilt-free about it. The right way to do it seemed to be buying almost the entire dessert menu."

Wyatt paid the bill once the waiter came around with our desserts in a to-go bag. I was too scared to look at it, and he didn't even blink at the new bill. He probably spent hundreds of dollars on us, which didn't phase him. It was refreshing but hard to relinquish the responsibility of paying the bill.

Tom took us back to the hotel, where we slipped into our pajamas, shared three desserts, and watched Food Network. Though, my pajamas were one of his famous white shirts. And when we fell asleep, our bodies willingly close, I didn't try to run away. I felt comfortable.

Chapter Twenty-One

Wyatt

I woke up with my arms wrapped around Hannah's waist. She was still asleep, cutely drooling on the expensive, white, Egyptian cotton pillows. I smiled to myself and took a mental picture before slowly removing my arm and turning the other way, so she wouldn't feel horrible about waking up knowing that we had cuddled throughout the night. I knew she wasn't much of a cuddler. I think she struggled with physical affection altogether, even if she wasn't quite aware of it.

I decided to sneak out of the room and head down to the restaurant that served us breakfast. We had it paid for but hadn't used it yet. I ordered a simple breakfast of eggs, hash browns, toast, and sausage. I knew she was a simple breakfast person and hated waffles but somehow liked pancakes. I even brought her orange juice.

When I returned to the room, she was awake and coming out of the bathroom. She looked exhausted, but exhausted looked cute on her. Her eyes widened when she saw what I was carrying, and I couldn't help but smile.

"Please say some of that is for me," she said with a groan.

"Of course. I didn't get two plates for myself." I handed her one and joined her at our breakfast nook attached to our small kitchenette. She downed the food like she hadn't eaten in days.

"I think I had too much wine," she said when she finished eating. "I'm going to go shower. I figured we'd head to the pool in a few hours."

"Sounds good to me." To my surprise, she came out of the shower in her bikini. Then, she covered it up in a black swim-cover dress.

After a few hours of us doing work on our separate laptops, which we agreed was okay since we had nothing else to do, we took the elevator up to the pool. Once we were in the pool, I didn't tell her how terrifying it was to me.

The pool was designed to look like it didn't actually end when it did. Because of the clear glass at the edge, and the height of the building, we had an incredible view of the city. I just happened to be afraid of heights.

She must have sensed what was going on because when she walked up to the edge and I stopped, she turned to me and giggled. "Is Wyatt afraid of heights? And here I was thinking you had no range of emotions."

"We're just...really high up," I responded.

She walked towards me in the water and took my hand in hers. "I'm scared of heights, too, Wyatt. This view is incredible, though. I won't let you fall." Even though I should be the one comforting her, her words and gestures were soothing to me, and I followed her to the edge.

It was only eleven, so the rooftop hardly had anyone there. I was surprised that the bar was even open. The pool extended through most of the rooftop, leaving space for chairs and cabanas on the sides.

She placed her forearms on the top of the glass and leaned her chin down on her arms. "It's so magnificent," she said, looking at the city in our view.

"Yeah, it is," I said. She didn't notice I was looking at *her*. The city view was decent, too.

"The lake cruise should be fun," she said when she turned around and noticed me watching her. I looked away, my sight switching to the city skyline.

"Yeah. I keep meaning to do one in Chicago, but I just get so busy."

She looked at me and laughed. "You, busy? Doesn't seem right," she teased, smiling as she looked down at the view below us. The view I refused to look at. Instead, I pretended we weren't extremely high off the ground, held together by a glass edge.

I turned to face the other direction where the bar was, and when I did, I felt water hit my back.

"Did you just…splash me?"

"Maybe. What are you going to do about it?" she questioned, smirking as she slowly started walking away in the pool, but the resistance didn't let her walk quickly enough.

I walked towards her, scooping her into my arms like a child would be held. She wrapped her arms around my neck, and we made eye contact. "Don't you dare, Wyatt Maverick," she warned. Her trying to be threatening was adorable.

"You splash me, then ask that I don't retaliate?" I kept my face straight and blinked a few times, but inside I was smiling. I acted like I was preparing to throw her under the water.

"Okay, okay, I'm sorry," she pleaded. "It was just a splash!"

I set her down and let her walk away before splashing her from behind unexpectedly. She turned towards me and glared.

I smirked. "It's just a splash."

We spent an hour exploring the long pool, and when it started filling up, we decided to rent a cabana and spend some time there relaxing. The weather was beautiful outside. One of the perks of being in Florida when it was cold up north. They brought us a drink menu, but we figured we didn't want to drink this early and instead requested a lunch menu.

I ordered a platter of expensive ass seafood, knowing she'd eat it if I bought it. She was a frozen fish person, so I ordered her fresh breaded cod.

"I'll give you a hundred dollars to try a crab leg right now," I challenged her.

"I don't want your money." I had to sweeten the deal, but what would entice her?

"I'll let you take a cute picture with me for Instagram. It'll drive Brad insane, too."

One of her brows furrowed, and she grabbed a crab leg from the platter and bit into it. Once she started chewing, she looked like she wanted to throw it up immediately, but she didn't. She finished her entire bite. "That was fucking disgusting, Wyatt. I will get revenge. First, I'll get my picture."

She stood up from the table and grabbed her phone, and I followed her. She took us back into the pool, handed her phone to a mom she started talking to, and then walked back over to me. She turned me so the background was the city.

"Okay, so here's what we're going to do. I'm going to use my hair to cover your face while you hold me in your arms. We're going to be really close to each other. I apologize."

"Jump on up," I told her. She leaped into my arms, her legs wrapping around my waist and my arms holding her up by the thighs. She giggled once she placed her forehead on mine, her hair engulfing me. We were so close that I could feel her breath on my face, and it felt incredibly sensual.

"Okay, got it," the woman called out.

She pulled away a few inches, and we locked eyes as she looked down at me, and I looked up at her. Her fingers ran through my messy, wet hair, and her lips parted. I would've kissed her right then and there, but I didn't want to scare her off. I wanted to know she wanted me the same way I wanted her. I wanted to know that her heart was skipping a beat like mine was now. That her breath hitched the same way when our eyes locked.

"Great, thank you," I called out to the stranger, letting Hannah jump out of my arms and grab her phone.

"Yes, thank you so much. My husband and I are grateful. It's our honeymoon." Her conversation with the woman took me by surprise. It was something about the way she emphasized husband and winked at me. It had an effect on me, one that stunned me into silence. "I believe we've got food to get back to. A lot of it." She brought me out of my trance.

Chapter Twenty-Two

Wyatt

Hannah was never the girl that took too long to get ready. She perfected her routine and almost had it down to a science. She said we needed to return around three thirty, so we left the pool area around two. We returned to the hotel room together and fought for the bathroom space to change. I let her win, and I changed into regular clothes in the room as fast as possible so that she wouldn't walk in on something accidentally.

The only nice tuxedo I had with me, besides the one from the wedding, was the one I wore to dinner last night. I needed a new one for tonight since we were going on an expensive dinner cruise she paid for months ago. I knew Hannah was excited about it and didn't want to give up the tickets.

"I think I need to get a tuxedo. Do you want to come with me to the store?" I asked her. Hannah loved shopping, and I'd get her a dress, too. I'd say she could get pajamas too, but I liked the idea of her in my shirts, so I secretly hoped she wouldn't look for any. She hadn't so far.

Her eyes lit up when she processed the question. "Absolutely, I do. Do you even have to ask?"

I smiled. Making her happy always made me happy, even if I didn't get to do it much. I didn't realize how much my words and actions had accidentally hurt her. I was trying to keep my distance, but I made her think I hated her. I hoped this trip was making up for that behavior.

I let Hannah find us a store that would have both of the things we needed, and the one she found was only a few blocks away, so we decided to walk together. Being from Chicago, we were used to walking to places. Every city needed a public transportation system as great as ours. We didn't need cars because we could walk a few blocks away and catch a bus or train, then get dropped off within a few blocks of our destination.

"It's humid out here, but it's so sunny and beautiful," I remarked on our walk. The weather felt different when we were sitting in a pool. Walking made me highly aware of the humidity and temperature.

"It truly is. Florida was always one of my favorite vacation spots. I've been to Destin, Panama City Beach, Miami, and a few more. And, of course, I came here before, for Disneyworld."

"I like to think that if I didn't choose to become a doctor, I'd travel the world," I blurted out. I didn't know if it was actually my goal to travel, or if it was something that was supposed to be everyone's goal. Truly, if I wasn't a doctor, I'd probably be an accountant.

"So, why'd you become a doctor?" she asked. "And you can still travel. You can make the time. You just can't be stubborn about accepting help."

"It was something I was good at."

"Most people choose a career they're passionate about." She said it so quietly I almost didn't hear her.

"I was good at it, but I also wanted to do something worthy. I hoped it would get my parents off my back and help them accept that I didn't want to go into accounting or work for my father, but they just didn't understand." I had never gotten this deep with anyone before, but the words couldn't stop flowing. She was so easy to talk to.

Thankfully, the conversation stopped when we entered the store: a local boutique that carried a designer she loved. She looked at the dress like a kid in a candy store. Her eyes lit up like Christmas lights, her entire face bright when she looked around. I imagined it was her own little heaven.

"Welcome," a woman greeted us. She had a giant smile on her face. She made a commission, so of course she did.

"I'm going to look at dresses," Hannah said before wandering off.

I handed the woman my credit card. "Whatever she wants, run it on this card. She's looking for a specific designer; ask her about it. I'll be finding myself a tuxedo." She walked off to greet Hannah at my direction, and I watched them engage in friendly conversation before I decided to look around.

I went with a simple black tuxedo with an elegant design and a high price tag, and I watched from the sidelines to determine what tie to get. Blue, to match her dress.

"It's already been covered, ma'am," the store clerk told her when checking her out.

Hannah looked around with wide eyes until she found me, then they turned to anger, only briefly. I walked up to the counter and handed my stuff over to pay. "Thank you, Wyatt." I was surprised, but I'd take it. I didn't see her dress beyond the color, but I couldn't wait to see her in it soon. She'd look great in anything.

Chapter Twenty-Three

Hannah

The cocktail dress I chose to wear to our dinner on a lake made me feel like a Cinderella since it was the same shade of blue. Mine was short, lying halfway down my thigh, with transparent mesh, off-the-shoulder sleeves. The top of the sleeves tied into small, cute bows.

I changed in the bathroom while Wyatt changed in the other room. I took the time to throw my hair into a pony with curled ends, put on red lipstick, and put on a tinted moisturizer to even out my skin tone. I was grateful for my eyelash extensions. It saved a lot of time to not hassle with glue, and I woke up feeling naturally pretty.

I looked at myself in the mirror to ensure I looked exactly how I wanted before leaving the bathroom. I had given Wyatt enough time to change, so I hoped I wasn't walking into the room with him naked.

Not that he would be unattractive naked, but I was happy when I was greeted by a fully dressed Wyatt who looked more like himself as he donned a tight-fitting suit that enhanced his already nice body. The suit showcased the muscles on his arms and thighs and made other places look nice that I didn't want to think about.

"You look beautiful. Fantastic. Spectacular," he said with wide eyes and an ear-to-ear grin. I had never had a man use several words to describe how I looked. It was unexpected from him, but it felt good to feel beautiful and appreciated.

"You don't look so bad yourself," I said.

"Before I forget, a gift for my lovely date," he said, grabbing a bouquet of flowers from our small closet. I didn't even notice him bring anything in, meaning he had to sneak them in before and keep them there. The sunflowers were already in a vase with water. "Your favorite, right?"

I nodded. "Was it the sunflowers all over the room on our first night that gave it away?" I asked with a chuckle.

"It was all the years you yelled at Brad for getting you roses on Valentine's Day when all you wanted was sunflowers," he said so low it was almost hard to hear him.

"I'll order our Uber now. The boat starts boarding at five," I said, turning away and burying my face in my phone to avoid looking at him. My heart started to beat abnormally when I looked at him, and I needed it to reset.

* * *

The Uber only took four minutes to arrive, so we left to go downstairs immediately after I ordered it. The ride to the dock was another ten minutes. We were ahead of schedule, thankfully. I hated being behind or falling off schedule. I thought I could avoid it by going off the books for the trip, but since this was a planned event, it brought back my anxiety over time.

"It's beautiful here," he said as we walked towards the sign with the company name of our boat cruise. There were a few other people gathered outside that I could tell were with us by the way they were nicely dressed.

"It is. I love being anywhere around water, as you can tell by the condo I chose back in Chicago."

"Carol said you chose it because you wanted the high price tag," he said.

I couldn't help but burst out in laughter. "You call your mom Carol?"

"I'm not sure if I can call the woman who didn't raise me, despite staying at home, Mom. I had a nanny. You may be surprised, but I'm also not good enough for her, and I'm her son and a doctor. But she wanted me to be an accountant with the family and work with my dad."

I rolled my eyes. "Something is truly stuck up her ass," I said, a little too loud. I caught the eyes of people around me. "You're an adult, I'm sure you swear," I told the girl sneering at me.

"You sound like my kind of people," a woman said from behind me. I turned around to be greeted by a smiling, hand-in-hand couple. The woman was small, around my size, with a simple pink dress, and the man was at least a foot taller than her with larger muscles than I had ever seen on any human being. "I'm Melissa, and this is my husband, Adam," she introduced.

"I'm Hannah, and this is my fri...my Wyatt. My husband, Wyatt," I saved. I didn't need to keep up the act here where no one was around, but it was best to stick to our story no matter where we went. I could've sworn the corners of Wyatt's mouth lifted when I called him my husband. I quickly looked away to pretend I didn't notice, so we wouldn't have to acknowledge it later.

"I actually know who you are. I'm a follower," she explained, "You're why we decided to visit Florida. You talked about how much you and your husband loved coming here, but I swear his name started with a B. But you didn't name him often, so I must be mistaken."

"It's so great to meet you!" I said. I was beyond thrilled to meet a follower. And she was visiting a place I talked about, which was all I ever wanted from travel blogging.

"Yeah, he doesn't like to be on social media much, but he promised to be active for our honeymoon coverage. I needed people to believe he's real, of course," I said, playing it off.

"Wyatt Brandon is my name. Sometimes I'm called Brandon," Wyatt chimed in to save my ass, though she already doubted herself anyways, and we could've gotten away with avoiding it.

"YES! That sounds so familiar now," she said.

"Ladies and gentlemen, we are prepared for you to board the boat for dinner now. Please have your tickets ready when you reach the gate," an employee said as they opened the gate. The people around us started to form a line, and we followed them, standing behind the sneering lady and in front of Melissa and Adam.

"Tomorrow, Adam and I are going to a private beach. You guys should come with us," she offered.

I shot Wyatt a glance to get a read on if he was interested. We were living it mostly day by day, so it wasn't like we had any plans.

"Sure, sounds fun," I agreed. Truthfully, I had no idea what we would do without the offer. I wasn't sure what Wyatt did in his free time or what he would enjoy out here. I certainly didn't expect he'd like pedicures, go-karting, and McDonalds.

"Great, here's my details," she said, handing me a business card.

We boarded the boat and were suddenly separated when they led us to our tables. There were three levels, each with only a few tables, setting us apart. The main level was an enclosed space, the second level was open, and the third was the exposed roof of the boat. All of them were decorated with elegant decorations and beautiful flowers. It was a romantic cruise, after all. We were on the middle floor.

"Here is our menu for tonight, Mr. and Mrs. Maverick," a waiter said, handing us a menu with three options for each course.

"We're about to eat good," Wyatt said as he looked at the menu.

"Do you like spinach artichoke stuffed mushrooms? We could split our appetizer. No way I can eat all this food by myself,' I said.

"Yeah, mark that down. I'll leave mine blank. I think for soup, I'm going to do French onion, lemon-crusted herb salmon for the entree, and triple chocolate layered cake for dessert. What about you?"

Wyatt's selections were the exact same ones. "Actually, same."

We handed in our cards when the waiter came around. Minutes later, he returned with soup and options for red or white wine or champagne, asking which we'd prefer.

"Red wine," Wyatt and I said simultaneously. It was getting weird how we wanted the same food and drink options. We laughed about it.

The wine and stuffed mushrooms were insanely delicious. The meal was definitely worth the twelve hundred dollars I spent on each ticket. A woman even serenaded us with a lovely voice as she played piano.

"Wow, this is absolutely incredible," Wyatt said as he tasted his salmon. I was still finishing my last mushroom, but he made me eager to taste the salmon.

"It better be, given the ticket price for this cruise."

"I can pay for my ticket if you want. You shouldn't have had to front all this yourself. I'm not sure how Carol can say you want my brother for his money when you pay for so much yourself."

"Absolutely not. You're my guest, Wyatt. I hope this has been a decent trip so far. A good replacement for the date you were supposed to have."

"Spending this time with you is better than anything another girl could've offered for the weekend," he said, causing me to briefly choke on the wine I was trying to drink. His flirting and compliments were always unexpected.

"The views are beautiful," I remarked, changing the subject. Outside, the sun was setting on the lake, and the water reflected pink. The lake was large, but we could still see the outline of beautiful, vibrant green trees that lined the lake. I was no stranger to lake cruises since I did every cruise Chicago had to offer, but this view without a city building in sight was something else to behold.

"Yes, the view is beautiful," he replied. I could see from the corner of my eyes that he was looking at me, not the landscape that surrounded us.

Dinner wrapped up as the sun was about to fully be unseen behind the trees. We had already started heading back towards the dock, and it didn't take long before we arrived. We were taken off the boat and started walking towards the street to catch a ride back to the hotel when Melissa and Adam walked up to us.

"You have to come out with us tonight!" she offered.

So far, we haven't experienced Florida nightlife. It seemed like it could be fun, and I was fifty percent sure Melissa wasn't a stalker or murderer. She couldn't murder me in public, at least.

"Sure," Wyatt offered up before I could even respond, "it seems fun."

"Yeah, what the hell. Certainly sounds better than going back and watching the cooking channel."

"Don't knock our favorite channel, Han. You know you love watching those intense cooking competitions," Wyatt called me out.

"Yes, of course, I'd never pretend I didn't, but I meant we're in Florida, on vacation...or, I mean, our honeymoon, and we should get out there and explore more."

"Eek! I know the perfect place," Melissa said, grabbing my hand and walking ahead of the guys.

Chapter Twenty-Four

Hannah

Since we went directly from our dinner to the bar, I was unsure if we were dressed appropriately. We walked probably half a mile until we stopped outside an elegant-looking bar with ambient lighting and dark, expensive decor that matched the bar's dark black and gold theme. Everyone inside matched us in wardrobe style. Suits and dresses.

We walked inside, and Melissa and Adam took us to seats at the edge of the bar. The seats at the bar were almost full, and the area had the best lighting in the place, with golden lights directly above our heads illuminating the area.

I didn't think it was possible to have cocktails that were more expensive than the ones at the hotel where my wedding almost took place, but Charming's, the bar we were at, had beat any place I had ever been to.

"They're expensive, but they're totally worth it," Melissa explained. She must've noticed my wide eyes at the drink menu. "First round is on me," she announced.

"Oh no, I couldn't allow that," Wyatt said. "They're on me." He took me by surprise, mainly because I was used to paying for everything. I still hadn't gotten used to Wyatt's constant offers to pay while we were in Florida.

I shrugged. "I won't say no to that," I said.

Melissa laughed. "Me neither, but I get the second round," she offered.

"I guess that means I'll take the third," I said.

"I'm going to cover all the drinks tonight," Wyatt decided, offering up his card to the bartender. "We'll take this one," Wyatt ordered, pointing to a picture of a beautiful blue cocktail on the menu. Below it, it said it was called the Sapphire Alpine. I had never had one before or heard of it, but it looked good, and the ingredients sounded like a fantastic blend of flavor.

I turned to Wyatt. "You don't have to. I can cover some."

"Let someone take care of you for once," he demanded in a quiet voice, quiet enough that our guests couldn't hear us over the sound of talking and the live piano player in the corner. While I was used to paying for most things myself, I wasn't exactly annoyed by it. I liked the idea of being in control. When I was younger, before I was the Hannah I am today, I had very little of it.

"Thank you, Wyatt. So what have you done in Florida so far? I saw the pedicures. I only wish Adam would go with me," Melissa said. She spoke fast, almost as if she was rambling about something, but I could clearly hear what she was saying. I assumed she was excited to be here with me.

"Well, on our first day, there was go-karting, mini golf, and Mcdonald's," I shared.

"And then there was the couples massage class and pedicures, and that sums up our short trip so far," Wyatt interjected, finishing off the description of our journey.

"We've only been here two days," I pointed out.

"Go-karts and McDonalds on your honeymoon, what an interesting time," Melissa said.

"We went to Bali for ours. It was only a few years ago, so it's still fresh.

Beautiful place. Have you been?" Adam mentioned. I had hardly heard him talk all night, but his wife didn't give him much time between her words and my responses.

"Bali was her first trip, sweetie," Melissa answered. "It was the first video of hers ever posted to her channel and first blog on her website."

It was weird to be around someone who could answer questions about my past before I could, but she was right.

"Actually, it was my first trip because it was so affordable. I didn't get offers for sponsored content until a year into my travel blog journeys. Then came the brand deals," I explained.

People often assumed I only traveled because I came from wealthy parents, but that wasn't the case. I worked hard, saved my money, and started it from my own income. Business school helped me learn how to grow myself and sell my potential, and it worked.

"I knew those trolls were wrong about you. You're too down to earth to be from a rich, pretentious family."

Wyatt laughed, presumably because of his family history. I wouldn't use the words down to earth to describe Wyatt. Or Brad. Or anyone in their entire family. Maybe she had a point.

"Melissa would know. Her dad is a congressman and career politician. Her mom is a celebrity publicist. It's the reason I married her. For the money," Adam said jokingly, and Melissa smacked him playfully on the arm.

"He's joking. I left my family's money behind after college. I made sure they paid for my education before I ran off on my own with my college sweetheart," Melissa said, looking at Adam in a way that I wished someone looked at me. A while ago, it was Brad who would look at me like that, with loving and longing eyes that he had for only me.

"So tell me, what is life like together back in Chicago?" Melissa asked, directing her question at Wyatt.

The bartender arrived with our drinks at the perfect moment, preventing Wyatt from answering the question. Melissa and Adam were distracted by the drinks, and the glance I gave Wyatt was unnoticed. We hadn't planned on what we'd tell other people when asked. He didn't know how much I shared with followers, but I hoped he knew enough about me and our life together to fake it. At this rate, I believed Melissa knew more about me than Wyatt and Brad combined.

Wyatt chugged a third of his drink before setting it down to answer the question. "We live near the beach, high up in a gorgeous condo, with our ferret named Ferret Bueller."

"Did the ferret have a day off?" Adam asked, making himself laugh.

I extended my leg to lightly kick Wyatt in the shin, but instead, Adam made a pained face and said, "Ow!"

"My bad, I thought I was hitting the table's leg, not yours," Wyatt said, taking the blame for me. He had to know that I meant to kick him. The ferret lie was so out of nowhere, and I wasn't sure I'd be able to keep up with it.

I started to chug my drink, and Wyatt ordered more before we were even finished. I knew tonight was awkward for both of us, but at least it wasn't more awkward than Wyatt's fingers grazing my thigh earlier.

"Yeah, we used to live with his annoying brother who had no care for anyone, just for himself. Remember that time he brought over a girl at one in the morning when we were asleep?" I questioned, referencing something Wyatt often did. It was the only vice he had. The only bad thing he did as a roommate, considering he spent most of his days working and had no time to do things that regular people did.

"Darling," Wyatt said, his hand folding over mine on the table, "maybe we were the ones annoying him when we'd wake up at midnight and clearly let him hear what was happening, so he fought back by doing the same thing."

I could feel the heat rise to my cheeks. I had never known us to be remotely loud enough for him to hear, and he didn't complain, but it turns out it was because he was fighting fire with fire.

Melissa giggled. "And how did you two meet?"

I couldn't tell her how I met Wyatt, whose hand still held mine. I met Wyatt after dating Brad for three months. He brought me home to our first holiday together as a couple, and I met his entire family. My story with Brad wasn't exactly a romantic tale.

"Our first encounter was so small that I doubt she'd remember," Wyatt started, "my brother was visiting me, and we decided to go to the campus cafe between his classes and get breakfast together. "There was a girl looking down, buried in her books, and she walked right into me. She blamed me for the coffee that got onto her book. I saw her in my class two days later, never noticing her before somehow. She was beautiful, and I knew it was fate pushing us together. I also bought her a new book and went to class early one day, leaving it at her preferred desk. Five years later, we got married." He squeezed my hand.

Wyatt's story threw me off, and I sat silent for a moment, processing his words. He's describing a story that happened two days before I met Brad in class, but there was no way he could've known about it. It wasn't Brad that I encountered. He must have been there to watch it. I couldn't question him at the moment.

"You guys are so adorable," Melissa said.

"And how did you guys meet?" I asked quickly, making sure to change the subject so she wouldn't ask anything further that would pull apart our story. However, he still distracted my mind knowing about my first meeting with Brad. The way he looked at me when he told the story was the same way I imagined Brad would be while we told that story to people.

Adam laughed while Melissa buried her head in her palm. Our drinks came just as I finished my first one, and Melissa started to drink hers, seemingly preparing herself for the story she would tell.

"Can't we tell the story we made up?" Adam asked.

Melissa shook her head. "One night, Adam came over to sleep with my roommate at the time. Gretchen was her name. He stayed over and woke up in the middle of the night and went into the kitchen, and got lost on his way back to her room. He fell asleep next to me and assumed it was my boyfriend. I screamed when I woke up, but we kept in contact, and both were out of our relationships a month later."

My jaw dropped to the floor. I had never heard anything like it, and I couldn't imagine if something like that had happened to me.

"So what's the story you made up instead?" Wyatt questioned. It piqued my interest that they felt their story was so bad that they resolved to create a separate one to tell people.

"That we were introduced by two of our friends. It's half wrong," Adam said with a shrug and a chuckle.

I liked getting to know Melissa and Adam. They weren't like the people we generally made friends with. They were real, genuine people and fun to be around. People that weren't using me to increase their social media reach.

"How about one more round before we head back? We're headed to the beach at ten so we can have a nice beach picnic," Melissa suggested.

Wyatt and I exchanged a glance before nodding our heads. "Sounds great."

Chapter Twenty-Five

Hannah

"Well, that was a fun night," Wyatt said as we exited our Uber and entered our hotel. Melissa and Adam were staying down the street, so we shared a car and dropped them off first, making sure to exchange information to head to the beach tomorrow.

"Yeah, I agree. Never thought I'd say that about a night I spent with you," I teased.

"Odd. Most girls say that after a night spent with me," he said playfully with a grin. I rolled my eyes.

"Where did the ferret lie come from?" I questioned now that we were alone.

He chuckled. "It's not a lie, Hannah. I got a ferret when you guys moved out. I actually have two, since I got my ferret a ferret." I felt bad that I didn't know something so simple about Wyatt, yet he constantly revealed that he knew more about me than I ever thought.

"It felt nice to spend time with someone who tried to get to know me rather than trying to take pictures with me to gain more followers," I explained, happily changing the subject. Wyatt wasn't around Brad and me enough to understand our friendships or what it was like to go out and be recognized when it did happen.

"I noticed you didn't take a single picture when we were out tonight," he pointed out. I thought about it and realized he was right, which wasn't normal for me. I always took pictures. I was living in the moment tonight and not trying to put on a show for social media. And it was nice that Melissa never once asked for a picture.

'You surprised me tonight," I told him as we exited the elevator on our floor. The closer we stepped toward the room, the more sweat accumulated on my palms.

"Because I was so kind, charming, and handsome?" he asked with a hint of a chuckle on his lips.

I rolled my eyes, opening the door to the hotel. "No, because you knew details about a day you weren't involved in," I answered.

He breathed a heavy sigh like a weight was lifted off his chest. "Because I was there, Hannah." His eyes darkened when he looked at me. His back pressed against the hotel room door, and closed it.

I shook my head. "Not possible."

"God, Hannah, You are so oblivious sometimes," he said, stalking me like a lion toward a deer. His eyes focused on mine as I started to back up. He stopped when I was pressed against a wall. "It was me you ran into. You were so focused on your book, and you ran off before I could talk to you. I thought about you for a while, and the day my brother brought you home, it fucking hurt. I told him about you. I pointed you out. I was interested in you. And then, he went back to class, and he recognized you. And he's always gone for what he wants."

I blinked a few times as the realization set in. Wyatt was the guy I ran into at the cafe. He kindly replaced my book, and his brother went after me knowing all this. Wyatt kept silent for years to let his brother be happy. A whole different life started to flash in my mind. A life where Brad wasn't the one that pursued me, but instead, Wyatt found a way to. Brad took that choice from me and lied to me for five years. My head was about to explode. All that effort to keep me to himself, just to ruin it and cheat on me with a girl he only knew because of me.

"I...I don't know what to say," I admitted. It wasn't often that I was left speechless.

Wyatt crushed the silence by crashing his lips into mine. It was simultaneously the hottest kiss of my life and the sweetest. There was a burning passion as his tongue slid into my mouth, wrestling against mine. Wyatt's hands were at either side of my head as they pressed up against the wall, and mine finally settled on gripping his hips after the surprise left my body. It wasn't like I didn't think about kissing him for the past few days. He was the first to break the kiss, pressing his forehead onto the wall next to my head. "I'm sorry," he mumbled. "I've been thinking about doing that again since Nashville. I know that makes me a shitty brother."

"I think it makes Brad a shitty brother that he knew you were interested and pursued me instead. I'm sure he cheated because he wasn't truly interested in me. He just wanted what you wanted. He proposed because I said it was the next step we should take and pressured him into it," I said something he potentially already knew, given that Brad was his brother and probably trusted him with his secrets.

"God, Hannah. I didn't know how bad it was. You deserve so much better than him." Wyatt pushed himself from the wall, taking a seat on the edge of the bed that we'd have to share shortly. I wasn't thinking about that a minute ago. "Do you even know how beautiful you are? How smart, caring, kind, and fun?"

"Of course, I recognize the good qualities I have. Brad's the idiot, not me," I teased. "And don't apologize for kissing me. I liked it."

"Good, because I really want to do it again. A lot, if you'll let me."

"As long as you understand that what happens on vacation stays on vacation, I can't guarantee anything beyond this trip because I don't know what life will be like when we get back home. Right now, I'm swept up in the beauty and the romance." I walked towards him, settling myself in between his legs at the edge of the bed. I wrapped my arms around his neck, looking down at him with a smirk, hoping he'd agree to my terms.

He nodded his head. "I've waited so long for your attention, Hannah. I'll take what I can get."

"And about what you said earlier...I'm sorry you heard things between us, and I know how you felt now. I know how that must've felt. I understand why you reacted how you did, and I'm sorry for judging you. It doesn't make me better than you just because I remained with the same person. You're single and can enjoy your company with whoever you choose."

"And now I choose you," he said, flipping me on my back in one swooping motion, hovering above me with his elbows holding him up on the bed. "I want to take it slow, but that doesn't mean I can't spend the night kissing you until we fall asleep." He leaned down and kissed me gentler than before, a smile planted on my lips.

My lips pressed into his, and I wrapped a leg around his leg, bringing his body down against mine so he wasn't hovering anymore.

He let out a quiet groan. "If you keep doing that, I won't be able to take things slow," he warned, our lips hardly an inch apart. It made me smile, knowing how responsive Wyatt was to me.

"Maybe I don't want to take things slow," I suggested, honestly. I wanted to have fun. I wanted a vacation fling while I wasn't thinking too much about what my life would be like next week.

"I value you as a person, Hannah. I want to take things slow because I want you to realize how good we could be together. I want you to choose me in the end, to want to be with me, even if I have to wait another five years."

Chapter Twenty-Six

Hannah

Sleeping next to him was different than the days before. Wyatt and I fell asleep entwined together, which was a way I had never woken up next to someone. And I surprisingly didn't hate it. There was so much I still had to ask Wyatt about the past, but I didn't want to ruin things just as they were getting fun. It felt like we had a few secrets, but if I mentioned it and our conversation got deep, it could bring out shit I didn't want to hear.

I untangled our bodies and lay on my side, resting my cheek on my palm as I watched him sleep. He was so peaceful and hot when he couldn't speak and tease me. I thought this trip would be more awkward than it had been, but I felt free being here with Wyatt. And now that I knew the truth, everything made sense. Wyatt never hated me; he hated being around me and Brad when he knew the truth the entire time. He changed his attitude on the trip because he didn't have his brother around to worry about. His brother screwed up, and he had a chance with me. I still couldn't believe I was waking up in a heart-shaped bed with Wyatt Maverick.

"Good morning," he mumbled before his eyes opened. I had no idea how long he had been secretly awake, how long he had known I was watching him sleep.

Hopefully, he thought it was cute.

"Good morning," I replied. "I'm going to go shower. They'll be here in an hour," I reminded him. We were both probably nursing a headache and aching body from the shots last night. I just hoped that because he wasn't slurring his words last night, it wasn't the alcohol talking, and he truly meant the things he said and didn't regret any of it. I didn't.

"We can save water and shower together," he suggested in a groggy voice, rubbing his eyelids as he slowly sat up in the bed.

"You wish you were so lucky," I said, leaning in and pressing a brief kiss to his cheek. "But that's not to say it won't happen over the next several days…" I said suggestively before walking away.

Last night, we were so tired that I fell asleep after making out in our underwear. It was dark then, but now as I walked away, he could see me in my full underwear glory if his eyes were open wide enough and adjusted to the morning light.

I brought my bikini to the bathroom to change into after my shower. I had the cutest swimsuit dress I'd finally be able to wear, but I left that outside so Wyatt would have to see me like this first.

Since being in Florida with him, I realized I wasn't acting like the girl I was before, but I liked that about me. I liked the person that Wyatt brought out in me: a confident woman who wasn't afraid to have a little fun with no strings attached. The confidence showed in the bikini pictures I posted to my social media story, with the hashtag #BeachDay to share with my followers. The likes and replies were rolling in seconds later, with hundreds already viewing it. I had never posted anything like it before, even when traveling to beach locations before.

I wasn't insecure with my body. I was very secure. Nor did I judge people who did post pictures like that. The postings turned Brad off, saying it was for his eyes only. It brought down my confidence.

"Your turn," I announced to Wyatt as I exited the bathroom, grabbing my laptop from my bag and sitting on the bed.

"Holy wow," Wyatt said, eyes wandering all over my body. He was certainly awake now. He was out of bed, grabbing his clothes for the day and putting them in a pile on a table. He walked over to me, leaning down and placing a kiss on my forehead before walking away and into the bathroom without another word. I smiled to myself at the feeling it gave me in the pit of my stomach.

It felt like we went to bed as friends and woke up as a couple. The kiss was sweet and intimate, something entirely unexpected of the man who told my ex to break up with me at our engagement party. One way or another, I'd find out why he said that before I left the state.

I had started to think of ideas to write down from my trip for the full blog post that would come after, but now I had an idea for a second piece I'd write. One that I potentially could never post, but it would be fun to document.

I wrote *how I fooled around with my ex*-fiancé's *brother on my honeymoon* at the start of my blog draft. I had one wholesome story about my fun experience so far in Florida, but this one started talking about how great of a kisser Wyatt was and how I was using my ex's brother to get over him and have fun in the process.

No matter what Wyatt said, he was still a one-girl-a-week kind of guy until his actions proved otherwise. I believed he only wanted me for the week we were in town. We weren't living in a romance novel. It was what I wanted and needed, too. Someone to get lost in. Next week, he'd go back to being a busy Doctor who never had free time, and I'd be planning my next trip. Something I hadn't thought about yet, because I was planning to take months off to celebrate my new marriage. A fact that made me frown every time I thought about it, simply because I never imagined this happening to me. I never thought I was the type of girl a man would cheat on and betray the day of her wedding. But obviously, I failed at something in our relationship for him to look somewhere else.

I slammed my laptop shut at the sound of the bathroom door opening. What I didn't expect was a shirtless Wyatt to be standing there, facing me, with a towel around his waist, water dripping from his hair to his chest. I bit my lip at the sight of him, and given the smirk planted on his face, I could tell he noticed. He clearly didn't miss much. He's shown me that much over the past few days.

"Forgot my clothes out here. Got a little distracted," he said with a wink, grabbing his clothes from the table and heading back into the bathroom. I let out a deep breath when he closed the door, feeling relieved. If he saw what I was writing about him, he'd hate me. I used our experience to write a blog I knew would capture attention. It wasn't like he paid attention to my blog or social media.

Deciding not to risk further exposure, I slid my laptop back into my bag to continue my blog later. I knew I would write about dinner last night and our conversation afterward, but I needed to create more experiences with him to write about. I threw on my swimsuit cover dress just in time for him to exit the bathroom.

He frowned upon laying eyes on me. "Please say you'll take that off at the beach. I liked the view," he said, straight-faced, slowly stepping towards me. My breathing slowed, nervousness taking over. Everything with Wyatt was new; I hadn't done anything new in over five years.

"Of course. Too warm to be in a black dress all day," I responded in a hushed tone.

I backed into the dresser slowly as he took steps closer to me. His body was inches from mine, and when he leaned forward, my heart leaped from my chest. Seeing my body's reaction, he smirked, grabbing our packed beach bag from the dresser behind me.

"We should probably head downstairs to wait," he suggested. I nodded my head, my breathing returning to normal once he walked away, and I followed him down to the lobby.

Melissa texted while we were in the elevator, telling me that their rideshare was out front waiting for us. I stayed on the other side of the elevator and remained silent. When we were in the elevator last night, the nerves inside were crushing me. Now that I had spent my night kissing and cuddling him, the nerves turned to a sexual tension that was building in my core.

"You're being awfully evasive. Was last night wrong? Do you regret it?" Wyatt asked with his head angled towards me, his eyes worried.

"No, no. I really enjoyed last night. It's just a lot to take in, and we're about to go spend the day with people who think we're a married couple. I'm nervous."

He walked to my side, slowly caressing my arm. "I won't do anything you're uncomfortable with. I'll be as husband-y as you want me to be."

When we exited the hotel, there was a giant stretch limo outside. Melissa's top half was hanging out of the skylight with a bottle of champagne in the air. "Let's get this started!" she yelled before her body disappeared into the limo.

"Jesus, I thought these were extinct," I remarked as I sat in the spacious vehicle. It was so large that there was a bottle cooler inside with a few different bottles of champagne.

"We use an app with rideshares of luxury vehicles only, and this seemed more fun than the Range Rover option," Melissa said. "Now, we're celebrating, so time to drink." She poured two glasses of champagne and handed them to Wyatt and me.

"What are we celebrating?" I stupidly asked.

She laughed. "Your new marriage, silly. To married life," she said, prompting a clinking of glasses in cheers that felt like a lie. I smiled through it, pretending to be a new, happily married wife celebrating her honeymoon.

I chugged the glass, knowing I'd need the liquid courage to get through the day. "To our new marriage," Wyatt said, a hand landing on my knee and giving a light squeeze.

Chapter Twenty-Seven

Hannah

The ride to the beach was about an hour away, which was expected given our location. But when we arrived, the location was stunning. There were a few houses along the beach, but they were far apart. We walked to the back of one of the houses that looked somewhat abandoned but did have outside furniture, so someone stayed there at some point.

"I hope this person doesn't mind that our private beach is behind their house," I said.

"Well, technically, it's ours for the day, so we're the ones that would mind," Adam said. "There was an offer to rent the house with private beach space for a day, and we took it up, wanting the full Florida experience."

It was so kind that they could have had this place to themselves for the day, but they chose to invite us along. We walked towards the water until we set up our stuff where the waves wouldn't reach. We had a cooler full of alcohol and water, beach towels, and a tall umbrella Adam kept above himself as he lay on his towel in the sand.

"Adam burns easily. He prefers to be out of the sun, but does enjoy the beach and the outdoors," Melissa explained. She rubbed sunblock on him even though he was in the shade. "You want some?" she asked.

"I brought some for us," Wyatt said, grabbing some out of our bag that I didn't know was there. "I'm a doctor. Sun protection is important," he said, pouring some on his hands and rubbing it all over his body. "Want me to get your back?"

I nodded my head, biting my lip. "All protection is important, Doc," I teased, clearing my throat afterward when I remembered we were with company. Though, said company did think we were married.

"Might as well just rub it all over her body," Melissa suggested, causing my cheeks to turn warm. My eyes shot to Melissa, and she winked at me.

Wyatt walked towards me and stopped in front of me, getting down on his knees in the sand. "Spread your legs apart," he said, low enough for only me to hear. I listened to his command. My body always listened to his demands.

He rubbed the lotion into his hands before slowly using his hands to rub it up my legs on each side. The feeling reminded me of our couple's massage, his hands getting just as high on my thighs as before. When his hands moved up to my stomach, he stood up. He put more on his hand before traveling up my arms and slowly moving across my chest. His face was inches from mine, and he smiled down at me while I looked up to make eye contact with him.

"You know, there are rooms in there," Melissa said with a soft giggle.

"Melissa," Adam said. "It's just sunblock. Leave the poor newlyweds alone." He had a joking tone to imply he wasn't seriously arguing with his wife over us and sunblock.

I smirked, my head falling forward in a chuckle at how he spoke. Wyatt used his lotioned hands to grab my chin, pulling my head back up. "Can't forget the face," he said, gently caressing my cheeks and forehead.

"Kiss her already," Melissa pressured. My heart rate picked up in pace as our eyes locked. I could tell from the look in his eyes that he wanted to listen to her suggestion but didn't know if I wanted it. I reached up and set my hands in his hair to assure him that I was comfortable with it. He took it as all the permission he needed, leaning down and pressing his lips hungrily against mine like we were the only people on the beach. My hand got lost in his hair as his hands fell to my waist. I would've stayed like this for hours, but Adam clearing his throat reminded us that we weren't alone, and we pulled apart.

"The beach here is so peaceful and beautiful. Such clear water, too. If only I weren't afraid of the ocean," I said.

"You're a travel blogger and you're afraid of the ocean?" Wyatt questioned, one eyebrow cocked as he looked at me. For someone who knew the most random information about me, he didn't know my biggest fear. It wasn't the ocean itself. It was the unknown.

"I never go more than feet deep, and I keep a vest on when I'm on a boat just in case I fall in."

Wyatt grabbed my hand, pulling me towards the water.

"Oh no, no, no," I said, pulling myself away. "I'm not going towards the water."

"Don't you trust me?" Wyatt said with a playful grin, his hand still holding mine while we stood in place.

I shook my head. "No, because I know you."

"Trust me," he said, leaning down and grabbing me by my legs, throwing me over his shoulders, my arms dangling at his back.

"Nuh-uh," I protested. "Put me down!" I kicked my legs playfully, not actually wanting to harm him.

"Time to get over your fear, Mrs. Maverick," he said.

I could see ahead of us that we were close to the water and felt my heart pumping above normal. I closed my eyes, my brain telling me that if I couldn't see what was happening, I was safe. He started to let go of me, bringing me towards the water. When I opened my eyes, he was waist-deep in the water, and my feet were in as he slowly started to put me down. As he released more of me, I began to wrap my legs around his waist.

"You'd rather be wrapped around me than be in the water?" Wyatt teased, his fingertips digging more into my skin. It wasn't the only thing pressing hard against my body.

"I'm scared of the water more than I'm scared of you."

"You're scared of me?" He pulled his head away, tilting it as he looked at me with curious eyes.

"I'm scared of myself around you," I said honestly. Wyatt responded by catching my lips with his in a gentle manner, not like he was starving for me this time.

"Look at you, Hannah, you're in the ocean and doing just fine. You're getting over your fear." Wyatt went from an emergency room doctor to a therapist real quick, and had a winning grin planted on his face.

"Only because I'm hanging onto you for my dear life."

"And you can always hold onto me as long as you need," he responded, causing a fluttering sensation in my stomach.

"At least if a shark gets me, they'll get you, too. Then we go down together," I pointed out with a small grin.

"Sharks are incredible creatures and don't really care to eat humans. We're hardly in the water, Hannah. You're safe." He rolled his eyes.

Melissa and Adam started to walk towards us in the water. "Time to play chicken," Melissa announced with a devious grin.

Chapter Twenty-Eight

Hannah

Our day at the beach was so perfect that I didn't want it to end. We played in the water for an hour, and I even started to like it. But in reality, I just felt safe while attached to Wyatt. We had a few drinks and made sandwiches for lunch. I felt myself acting differently with Wyatt than I ever had with Brad. Like I wasn't trying to impress him and fit into his world. Instead, it seemed like he was trying to fit into mine.

Part of me felt bad for quickly shifting my affection onto Wyatt. Maybe I was burying myself in a distraction, but I wouldn't know until we got home. Wyatt was right with what he said to me before. I wasn't sad because I lost Brad. I wouldn't have brought Wyatt to Florida if I was truly torn up over our breakup. I wouldn't have kissed him last night, only a few days after my wedding was supposed to happen.

With the sun setting, as we made smores near the beach with our new friends, I felt more natural than I had for years now. We sat on the sand, my head resting on his shoulder, and it felt right. Relaxing, calming, and like something that would've happened if my initial honeymoon was still on. Sometimes things happen for a reason, but right now, I don't care to know that reason. I just wanted to enjoy the moment.

"We can drive back soon if you want, or if you don't feel like making the trek back, we have two bedrooms here," Melissa offered. We had spent the day drinking at our beach area, and it was probably best to stay here. I didn't make a post about the hotel today, but I'll make one tomorrow. At least I had fun material for my blog.

I took out my phone and snapped a picture of the sun setting over the beach before it fully disappeared behind the horizon. We were on the last bit of light left in the day.

"How do you feel about staying?" I asked Wyatt, pulling my head away from his shoulder and looking over at him.

"Let's stay, we're having fun, and we get to wake up with this view," he said what was on my mind.

I brought up my Instagram account and posted a picture of the sunset I had just taken. Surprisingly, I hadn't checked my phone all day. I had thousands of notifications. My story with my bathing suit was my most viewed of all time, and there were so many messages that I couldn't keep up. I groaned at the sheer amount of messages. I hardly ever let myself get behind before, but I was so wrapped up in our beach day.

Before putting my phone away again to enjoy our nighttime bonfire together, I devised a backup plan and sent Priya a text.

sos. need you. pls respond to my messages. mention how thankful i am and how i'm enjoying my honeymoon. thnx xoxo

I mostly responded to things myself to keep my blog and social media profiles authentic and genuine. It was my job, so it wasn't like I had anything else to do. But sometimes, I tapped Priya in to help me out. And I did pay her, though she said she didn't need payment. Priya was a stylist and took on well-known clients that paid good money so she'd work less and had free time to help out occasionally. I wouldn't trust anyone else with my accounts.

I braced for the lecture about how I was ruining the mood by posting the night on Instagram, but it never came. Everyone around me was calm and understanding, which I wasn't used to. I knew Melissa understood, but Wyatt was starting to surprise me.

"You're not going to scold me for working and looking at my phone while we're with friends?" I finally questioned. I didn't know why the words escaped my mouth.

"No, you're an adult, and I'm not your dad," he responded.

My mouth inches from his ear, I said, "You could be for a night if you wanted." I heard him gulp.

"We may be across from you guys, but I still heard that," Melissa said through her laughter.

"Pass the marshmallows," I told her as she gripped the bag tighter.

"I'm not done with them."

"You're literally just shoving your face with them. Just give me one to roast." I rolled my eyes. She handed me one, and I grabbed the metal roasting stick she brought, placing it over the fire.

"I think it's warm now. You can take it out," Wyatt said after a minute.

"That's ridiculous, it's not done until it's black all over. Everyone knows that." I scoffed at him.

"That's the grossest thing I've ever heard," Wyatt said.

Across from us, Melissa made a shocked sound.

"You can't knock it until you try it, Maverick," I teased. Once my marshmallow was beyond roasted, I set it down on my plate. "Open up," I directed.

While he shook his head, I took a bite and swallowed half of the marshmallow, looking at him with a smirk. I don't know what came over me next. Maybe it was how his eyes darkened when he watched me eat the marshmallow, but I fed it to him. I shoved a half-eaten marshmallow into his mouth. His eyes widened at the intrusion. When he finished swallowing, his lips pursed together, and his head nodded.

"I guess you have a point. That was good," he said. I felt his hand rest on my leg; it was the first time he held it there instead of rubbing the area with a lotion or oil. Somehow, it felt more sensual.

"I'm always right," I managed to say, prompting his laughter. "Tell me when I was wrong."

"Let's see," he said, tapping his chin, "how about when you said you liked the last Star Wars? Or when you said pineapple doesn't belong on pizza?"

"I liked it, and it doesn't," I said, defending my stance. "Not my fault. Your taste buds are weird."

"Adam's favorite is mushrooms and pineapples." Melissa grimaced.

"We just can't let them order the pizza," I said. Melissa laughed with me.

"It's early, but we're going to retire inside," Adam said, squeezing her shoulder, and I understood what he meant. "Let's show you to your room."

After throwing a bucket of water on the fire, we followed them inside, and they directed us upstairs and to the first door we saw. The room had a small, full-size bed. It was plain with no decorations and a gray and white theme.

"We actually fly out tomorrow, so we'll have to take you guys back around nine," Melissa said before leaving us.

"I realize now that we don't have anything to sleep in," I pointed out. All we had on us were our phones, wallets, and keys. We weren't expecting to stay.

Wyatt started to climb out of his clothes, leaving himself in his boxers.

"What are you doing?" I questioned, hoping he wasn't about to strip naked, especially not without an explanation.

He smirked. He handed me his shirt before speaking. "Here. Pajamas."

"I'm supposed to sleep in my underwear and a shirt?"

"I've seen you in less."

I felt the heat rush to my cheek at the comment. I was blackout drunk when he changed me into his boxers and shirt the other day. And he was a total gentleman. I pushed down my shorts, and he turned around. I took the opportunity to take off my shirt and swimsuit top and throw on his shirt while he undressed into his boxers. I bit my lip while looking at him, taking in the beautiful sight of him.

I don't know what took over me, but I grabbed his hand and led him to the bed, getting under the covers and laying on my side. "Cuddling would be nice right now."

Chapter Twenty-Nine

Wyatt

I thought about making my move. It would be the perfect time. Hannah was the one who brought me to the bed and pressed her back into my chest. Still, it didn't feel right yet. I wanted her to initiate it. I wanted to hold no doubt that she wanted this as much as I did. I wanted her to choose it, to choose me. For now, I'd at least enjoy sleeping next to her. Nothing said we had to go to sleep, though.

I brushed the hair from her neck, leaning down and kissing her delicate skin. I was cheating. I knew it was her weak spot, but I didn't intend for things to go too far unless she wanted it and initiated it.

Hannah turned over, laying on her back and twisting her head in my direction. "I kind of enjoy sleeping next to you," she said in a whisper.

"Kind of enjoy? Thanks for the glowing review," I teased. She whacked my chest lightly with the back of her hand.

"There are things I think I'd enjoy doing with you more in the bed," she muttered, a grin forming on my face in response.

"And what is that, Hannah?" I pushed hair behind her ear before cupping her cheek in my hand, my face gravitating towards hers until we were inches apart.

"Let me show you," she said, turning her body towards me and grasping the back of my neck with her hand, closing the gap between our lips in a kiss. With a sense of need, my tongue pressed for entrance past her lips, and seconds later, my tongue lapped hers. Unlike the romantic ones we had shared prior, our kiss was messy, rough, and greedy. Her taste and smell pleasantly filled my senses, and it was like heaven.

Hannah was the first to break the kiss, her hand remaining around my neck. "I want to be on the same page. Are you...are we...?" she started to ask but got lost in her words, her cheek flushing pink.

"Don't get me wrong, Hannah. I want you more than I've ever wanted someone in my life, but I don't think the guest bedroom of a house we're sharing with two people is the right place. And I will wait until you're sure you're fully ready. Before we have sex, we should discuss things, and have a conversation," I told her. She released a breath.

"I want you, too, but I'm nervous. I haven't been with anyone new in half a decade, and you, you're the brother of the man I was with for years, and I've heard you hooking up with other women, so I need to get out of my own head. But you're right, we should have a conversation before we have sex, so I can tell you things like how I'm on birth control and I hate missionary."

I groaned at her words. She was making my resistance wear thin, but at least we could do other things. I leaned over her, moving us so she lay below me, and I hovered on my hands above her. Moving lower on the bed, I pulled up my shirt that she was wearing, kissing a trail from her stomach to the top of her panties.

"You're right. You have heard me with other women. And I've heard you with the man who had you despite knowing how I felt, and it was torture. But since we lived together, I can confidently say that I can make you feel better than he ever could and make you forget anyone else came before you. You're all I see." I ended my speech by looping my fingers in the waistband of the pink lace, pulling them down slightly. "If you'll let me."

I looked up, and Hannah was biting her lip and frantically nodding her head. I grinned at her eager response.

"You deserve to be worshiped, Hannah," I told her before pulling them down entirely and tossing them on the floor. "and I'm going to worship you so hard that you can finally call me God," was the only warning I gave her before I buried my face in between her legs, my tongue pressing circles around her clit.

Chapter Thirty

Hannah

The way Wyatt ravaged me was unexpected and very, very hot. I didn't have the heart or the time to tell him I wasn't interested in that. Not only had I never had an orgasm that way, but Brad hated it, making me insecure about that and about myself. Wyatt squashed all of that in seconds. While his tongue worked my clit, he had me writhing beneath him already. His hand splayed across my abdomen to hold me in place, and I could feel his lips curl up into a smirk against my skin.

"Clearly, someone hasn't been showing you how fucking good you taste." His simple words made my heart race even more. He made me feel wanted, which I wasn't used to. I knew I should have been, but I let someone slowly destroy my self-worth over the years, and it took being with his brother to realize that.

Normally, I didn't care for any form of oral. Wyatt was an expert with his mouth, so much so that I already felt an orgasm building low in my abdomen. He had spent less than a minute with his tongue on my clit, and I was a mess. I was ready to shatter when two of his fingers entered me and curled to hit the right spot. I held back, wanting to savor the moment rather than have to stop before it even really began.

We made eye contact, and it was too much for me. His hooded eyes looked at me intensely, and I threw my head back, focusing on the ceiling instead. My hips bucked up, and I unintentionally rode his face. It almost felt like I wasn't in my own body. I had never felt this good. I didn't know it *could* feel this good.

"Wyatt," I moaned pleadingly, unsure what for. I could feel his lips curve into a smirk against my skin. He pulled away for a brief moment, and I missed his tongue.

"Does it feel good, Hannah?" he questioned. Something about how he said his name while my juices covered his face sent a spark of electricity throughout every bone in my body.

"Yes, yes, yes," I chanted.

He dove back in and flicked my clit with his tongue teasingly before increasing pressure and circling again. Once his fingers were inside to the last knuckle, and he curled them again, I shattered. My thighs began to shake, and my fingers found his hair, gripping tightly as I held his face in place.

"Fuck, Wyatt, that feels so good," I said breathily as my walls clenched around his fingers.

"And you taste so good, Hannah. Like a fucking dream."

His tongue licked through my folds when my shaking subsided, briefly entering me. Once his tongue left my body, I felt empty again. He brought himself on top of me, his length pressing into my stomach through his boxers as he brought me into a searing kiss. I tasted myself on his tongue and was surprised it didn't gross me out. I had never let someone kiss me after. I didn't expect to be so turned on after I had an orgasm, but I was. Wyatt's tongue fought mine as his erection only pressed deeper into me, setting a fire inside me.

"I want you, Wyatt," I whispered when I pulled my lips away from his. His breathing was heavy as he pressed his forehead into mine. "Please."

"I don't want you to regret it. You're just in post-orgasm bliss right now," he said, his fingers gripping my hips as his lips kissed down my jawline and neck.

"No," I said, shaking my head. "I want you so bad. I want to feel you deep inside me, *please,*" I begged. I could tell that Wyatt was big from feeling him against my stomach, and I wanted to feel him inside of me instead. I had only had sex with one man my entire life. I had a feeling Wyatt could bring me to new heights.

"I don't have a condom," he mumbled. I could hear his restraint withering in his voice.

"You're clean, right? I am, too. I'm on birth control, and I trust you." Maybe it was the desperation talking, but I felt the same way before he gave me an orgasm.

He nodded his head. "I've never gone without one before. For you, I would."

He shifted down and pulled himself out of the hole in his boxers, giving himself a few strokes that I felt against my leg. Before I could question what was happening, he lined himself up with my entrance and thrust inside to the hilt swiftly. I was so wet that it wasn't hard to do.

"Fuuuck," he groaned, burying his face in my chest. "You feel so fucking good." He ceased movements for a moment and focused on my nipple, his tongue flicking it a few times before he sucked a few times, ending with a bite. Once he removed his mouth, he hovered over me, leaning on his palms. He made eye contact with me and, with parted lips, started to move his hips again. He'd pull back to the head before pushing back inside, so I was full of him. Every inch buried inside of me in slow, steady thrusts.

"Wyatt," I whispered, my fingers digging into the skin on his back. "Harder, please."

He pulled out of me and tugged me up, rolling me so I was on my stomach instead. "You hate missionary, right?" he repeated, taking my hips in his hands and pulling them up so my ass was in the air, facing him. I was glad he couldn't see my face because my cheeks were red and hot. I hadn't ever been in this position before.

"That's a good girl," he said when I was in position. My face reddened, but I liked what he said. Due to what I read, I was pretty sure I liked dirty talk and praise, but I never experimented before. I didn't feel comfortable asking Brad to try something new. Wyatt was bringing me new experiences without me having to ask, and the slight domination in him drove me wild inside.

I braced myself on my forearms, my head buried in the pillow as he entered me again. His thrusts were harder this time, and he managed to go deeper while simultaneously hitting the perfect spot. I officially loved this position. I had never tried anything beyond missionary, which was how I knew I hated it.

Wyatt's hand grabbed my hair into a fist, and he pulled it back, gently pulling my head up from the pillow. He brought my back to his chest, his hand holding my throat but not squeezing tight. He turned my head to face him, bringing my mouth into another frantic, wild kiss where our tongues raged against each other. His kiss swallowed my moans and he groaned into my mouth in return.

When he pulled away from my mouth, he pushed my long hair to my left shoulder, exposing the right side of my neck to him. He bit the side of my neck, and I leaned my head back into his shoulder, my right arm reaching behind me and cupping the back of his neck. "Just like that, Wyatt."

My words made his hips push harder into me, and each time he was to the hilt, he circled his hips for a moment before thrusting again.

"You feel too good, Hannah. I can't last," he said. His hand reached in front of me, and his fingers began to work my clit again, placing pressure in circles. My hands tugged at his hair as the sensations of pleasure overwhelmed me. I knew he was close when his thrust became deep and rough.

He buried his face in my neck and moaned my name repeatedly, followed by a string of curses. When he came, he thrust so roughly to bury himself deep inside me, forcing a small scream of his name out of me as my second orgasm washed over me. Two more than I was used to. He stayed seated inside me for a moment while we caught up on our breathing. He then slowly pulled himself out of me and sat on the edge of the bed. I flipped to lie on my back, and he looked over at me with a smile.

"Let's go clean up together," he suggested. Before I could ask a question or answer, he left the room, and I heard a bathtub filling with water. He reappeared a second later, leaning on the door frame and smirking.

"We're going to...take a bath? Together?" I questioned. He nodded his head and managed to make the gesture look sexy.

I sat up from the bed and followed him into the tub. It was warm and full of bubbles. He sat in first, then let me sit between his legs, my back against his chest. It was the perfect temperature and so comfortable. I had never taken a bath with anyone before.

He used a washcloth and the bubbles in the tub to wash me, and I smiled as I leaned back into him. It was such a sweet gesture. After he finished, he washed my hair for me, massaging the shampoo in. The simple gesture made me moan in pleasure. It felt like going to the salon and getting a head massage in the bowl, but better because the touch came from Wyatt.

"You make that feel really good," I told him.

"I'm glad. I've never done this before. But if you don't stop with those noises, this bath might turn from sweet to sexy real fast," he threatened in a sultry tone, causing me to bite my lip.

"Me either," I admitted. "I...I'm not used to being cared for after. Thank you, Wyatt. I'll keep my noises down, because I don't have another round in me," I admitted with a giggle. He rinsed the shampoo from my hair after a long head massage, then he conditioned my hair.

When we were done, and it was time to get out of the water, he wrapped me in a towel and dried me off. I had never felt so cared for in my life. Afterward, we fell asleep in each other's arms at the beach house.

Chapter Thirty-One

Hannah

"It was so nice meeting you," I said to Melissa while we said goodbye. She brought us back to the hotel by nine in the morning since she and Adam had to catch a plane today. Beyond friends I had since before my business, I didn't have many people I connected with like I did with her. We were already excited to meet again in the future, and I hate that we met so close to her leaving town.

We hugged outside of our hotel, and Adam and Wyatt shook hands.

"Congratulations to you both again. You're so cute together," Melissa said with a wink.

I grabbed onto his hand and squeezed it. I woke up happy about what happened the night before and had no regrets. We hadn't talked about it yet, but the entire day was free with no plans.

"It was great meeting you guys," Wyatt said. "We'll get together again sometime soon."

We waved as they drove off to the airport, and then we dropped hands. I was surprisingly sad at the loss of his hand.

"What do you want to do today?" Wyatt asked.

"First, I need to work a bit on some travel content. I figured we'd visit the hotel's in-house restaurant tonight and review it. I need to post more about the hotel since we spent yesterday away."

"While you do work, maybe I'll relax and read a book," Wyatt said.

We smiled at the staff on our way in, then took the elevator to our room. Today, I was thankful for the massive heart-shaped bed. There was enough room for me to type on my laptop secretly and for him to read without being able to see my screen. I continued writing my blog post while he read a mystery novel.

"I didn't take you as a reader. I guess I had never seen you with a book," I remarked while on a break from writing.

I had written about how Wyatt and I hooked up for the first time and how incredible it was. My story began with finding out Brad was cheating, going on the trip with Wyatt, and how he confessed to knowing me. I talked about the first kiss. I wasn't even sure I would post it, but writing about it made me happy. If anything, I'd have it in writing to remember forever. No matter what happened between us, I didn't want to forget.

"You won't see me reading romance novels anytime soon, but I do love Lee Child novels and Brandon Sanderson."

"I used to love reading," I remarked.

"You don't anymore?"

"I don't have the time." I shrugged.

"What are you working on over there?" he asked, peeking over. I slammed my laptop shut.

"It's a secret," I whispered. He chuckled and shook his head.

"I get it, I get it," he responded before returning to reading his book, shifting back to his side of the bed. Feeling like I had written enough for the day, I set my laptop aside and picked up my phone instead. I used the time to respond to some comments on my various profiles and posted a picture of Wyatt buried in his book. He immediately racked up the likes. His face wasn't even visible, but my followers loved him anyway. I smiled to myself while reading all of the comments talking about him, despite the ability to only see his wild set of hair.

"Your head is very popular with the ladies. Kind of like your butt in pants," I said, laughing.

I noticed him shaking his head but refusing to look up from his book.

"So, about last night," I said, and he looked up from his book. He marked his spot, then closed it, setting it on the nightstand. His eyes almost looked worried, like he thought I was going to say something bad.

"What about last night?" he asked in a soft tone.

"It was amazing. I had never...orgasmed from being eaten out before. I certainly never orgasmed twice before." I could feel the heat rising in my cheeks.

Wyatt sat up in bed, leaning towards me and cupping my cheek in his large, soft palm. "You are amazing, Hannah." He brought his lips to mine in a gentle, soft kiss that was somehow still full of so much passion. It wasn't the type of kiss that led to sex. It told me how he felt without words. But even without sex, every kiss from him was hot enough to turn me on.

I almost wanted to say fuck the restaurant tonight, and order in-room service and spend the time by ourselves. We only had days left of our vacation, and I wasn't sure if any of this would continue outside of Florida. I told him I wanted a vacation fling only, but I said that to protect myself from being hurt again. Part of me knew Wyatt would never hurt me, but I still struggled. I thought Brad was a safe bet, too.

"I'm excited for tonight. I heard this place has amazing steak," I said, changing the subject.

"Yeah," he said with a chuckle. "That's definitely what I'm thinking about right now. Juicy, warm, wet steak." He winked while I rolled my eyes at him.

With a few hours until we had to go down to dinner, I decided to respond to a few emails while Wyatt finished up his reading. I didn't need much time to get ready, so I let him use the shower first. He never took more than ten minutes, anyway.

I used the time he was in the shower to call Priya so I could update her. He couldn't hear me over the water, so I called her immediately after he got in. She picked up on the first ring.

"Two calls in one vacation. I'm lucky to get your attention. What happened? Gimme the deets, Han," Priya said. I rolled my eyes and wished she could see.

"I have some news," I said, working up the courage to tell her what happened.

"You boned Wyatt!" she screamed.

"Shut up," I said, but I didn't deny what she had just screamed. Hopefully, she was alone and not with anyone we knew. Everyone would know who she was talking to and who she was talking about.

"So, that's a yes, right?" she said in an eager tone with a pitch higher than normal.

"It's a yes," I said, then sighed. Priya was the only one I trusted enough to tell this information to.

"Oh my God, how was it? I bet he's amazing. Is he amazing?" She talked way too fast, but I still understood every word. She squealed with joy at the end, too. She was never like this when I talked about Brad and I should have seen the signs about my relationship then. If Brad was good for me, my best friend would've been happier.

"It was fantastic. He actually made me orgasm, and then he washed me in a bath. He's better than I ever imagined."

"So you admit it. You did imagine it before." Well, she caught me there. There was still something I didn't tell her.

"The night of my bachelorette party, when we got smashed, and I went to the hotel to rest before Brad saw me like that, Wyatt ended up in my room. I thought he was Brad, and we kissed. It was incredible. I knew it wasn't Brad then, but I kept going. I confirmed it by grabbing his hair, and I had to pull away because I felt guilty. I thought it was only the alcohol affecting me, but I no longer think that's true," I explained. I felt so terrible over what happened that I hadn't even told Priya. I was going to, eventually.

"Bitch, there's no way you kissed Wyatt a few weeks ago and didn't tell me, your maid of honor and best friend of like two decades" she said in a jokingly bitter manner.

"I'm sorry. I was processing what happened, but I swear I was going to tell you. Eventually." I heard the water turn off. "I've got to go, Priya. He's out of the shower. I'll text you soon." I hung up the phone.

She texted me a moment later.

Of course you gotta go when he's out of the shower...;)

I sighed. I should've kept my mouth shut, but Priya was my best friend, and I needed to tell someone.

"Shower is yours," Wyatt said as he walked into the room with a glistening chest and a towel wrapped around his waist.

After my shower, I picked out a cute olive-green summer dress. Most of my wardrobe for this trip was dresses, swimsuits, and lingerie, so I didn't have many outfit options. A summer dress at a nice restaurant fit well, too.

For makeup, I decided to put on lip gloss, concealer, and a hint of blush and call it a day. My eyelashes were still done from the wedding, and I didn't need much makeup to feel good about myself. I felt more free wearing less, especially being on vacation in a humid state.

It was a crazy change in the past few days since before. I wouldn't be caught dead out without a lot of makeup. I needed matte lipstick, contour, bronzer, foundation, eyeliner, and a fun, colorful eye look. Makeup was fun and truly a form of art, but I focused on bringing back a renewed sense of confidence without the clothing and makeup I constantly wore.

"You look stunning," Wyatt said as I twirled in the dress.

He wasn't wearing a suit, but he still looked nice in his tight-fitting black Dickies, and his tucked-in, button-up white shirt. His sleeves were folded over, and his Rolex was showing. I hardly saw him in it, but I knew it was a gift from his dad.

"You don't look so bad yourself," I said with a small smile.

We walked down to the restaurant together, and when I looked around, I was thankful we had a reservation. It was a nice, dimly lit restaurant with a full house inside. The tables had flowers and lit candles.

"Right this way," the server told us. Then, she led us to a small table in the back, away from the rest of the crowd. It was the restaurant's darkest corner, which wasn't a coincidence. It was our honeymoon, after all, and that was known around here. Of course, they thought we wanted a private dining experience.

When we sat down, I took pictures of the table decor and menu before I even opened it to read it.

"What do you think you're going to get?" I asked Wyatt as I perused the menu.

"The Wagyu Filet Mignon, with brussel sprouts and broccoli," he answered, his gaze not leaving the menu.

"I don't know what I want."

"You were talking about steak," he reminded me.

"Because I know you like steak," I admitted. This would be a test of Wyatt's true knowledge of me. "I feel like I should be eating some of their expensive options like steak or lobster."

'But you like chicken tenders and fries," he said with a proud grin. Bingo. No matter how much money I had or the clothes I wore, I was a simple girl when it came to food. Money couldn't change your taste buds.

"Maybe I should take a picture of your food so I don't look weird to my followers."

"If your followers would think less of you for enjoying chicken tenders, then they don't deserve to follow you," he said.

Sure, it wasn't as exciting for a picture, but at least I'd be honest about the food and what I liked. I agreed with what Wyatt said and decided it was for the better.

"Have we decided what we want to eat?" the waiter asked.

"Yes," Wyatt answered. "I'll have the Wagyu Filet Mignon with brussel sprouts and broccoli, and she'll have the chicken tenders and fries meal." He looked over at me. "With ketchup, please."

The waiter smiled at us before walking off.

"I knew if I didn't order for you, you might chicken out on ordering what you wanted. Pun intended," he said with a smile. With no menus to hide us, we locked eyes instead, smiling at each other and sitting in silence for a minute. Wyatt constantly knew what I wanted before I did and potentially knew more about me than I knew about myself.

"You, Wyatt Maverick, are a good man. Deserving of the best things in life."

"Only of those best things in life is sitting across from me."

I felt the heat rising to my cheeks. I wasn't used to someone being so forthcoming with compliments. Brad complimented me, but he had a way of sandwiching insults between compliments, which drove me insane. Sometimes I wanted to hear that I'm pretty, not that I'm pretty despite the color of my top not looking good with my skin.

Our food didn't take long to arrive, and I took a few images of my meal before digging in. I wasn't trying to impress anyone when I ate here, so I didn't fear how I looked when I gobbled up my dinner impressively fast. The chicken tenders were delicious, crunchy, and juicy, while my friends were homemade and seasoned to perfection. I took a picture of Wyatt's dinner, too, not because I intended to post it instead of mine but because I intended to post it with mine. I even included his dressed torso in the background to show us out on a date.

"You must've really liked your meal," Wyatt said as he finished his meal, nodding to my already-cleared plate.

"They managed to make a simple meal elegant and delicious. I hope you liked your food."

"The meat is tender and flavorful, and the sides have been seasoned to elevate them. It's delicious."

When we got the check, Wyatt handed over his card, and I managed to hold back from protesting and allowed him to pay.

After dinner, we walked back to the room and decided to have one inside night watching television instead of going out and doing anything else. We still had a few nights in Florida, and more exciting things to do, too.

At first, we stayed on our sides of the bed, but then I leaned my head against his chest, and he wrapped his arm around me. We watched Parks and Rec, which was a favorite series for us both. I couldn't remember the last time I laughed so much while doing something as simple as watching television with someone.

When a commercial break came on, I sat in Wyatt's lap, placing a leg on either side of him. "There's something I want to try that I've never wanted to try until now," I said, leaning down and placing kisses along his chest. I made eye contact through my lashes.

He smirked. "And what is that, Hannah?" Christ, I loved the way he said my name. When he was turned on, his voice had a deep rasp to it, and it sounded sexy coming from his mouth. I was never particularly into my name before Wyatt said it and moaned it on our vacation.

I trailed kisses down his stomach, the fuzz tickling my mouth, and stopped above his boxers. He slept in his boxers, so it was natural that we were cuddling half-naked, too. By now, I had seen him fully naked and felt comfortable and confident around him.

"I've never had, or wanted, a cock in my mouth until now," I told him, biting my lip as I looked up at him, our eyes meeting again. My fingers slipped into the hem of his boxers, pulling them down to reveal an already hard Wyatt. The thought of my mouth on him was enough to turn him on, which did something to my ego. I wasn't used to holding this kind of power over men.

"Are you sure?" he asked, looking down at me with wide eyes. I answered his question by placing my hand on his shaft and licking circles around the head of his engorged cock. He tasted sweeter than I expected, even with the salty precum that leaked from his tip.

I wrapped my mouth around his cock and pushed down until the tip was fully inside. He was big, making it a tight fit, but it was worth it. I never craved someone so bad before. I wanted to show him that I was as enthusiastic as he had been when he did the same to me. He didn't have to - I figured most men don't - but he did.

His hips pushed up, sending another inch in my mouth, as his hand tangled in my hair. I could tell he was holding back and trying to be gentle. Presumably, he knew it was my first time. Either he had a suspicion about his brother, or my inexperience was showing.

"You're doing so good," he cooed, making me want to do better. Blow jobs were supposed to be sloppy, right?

Once I felt comfortable with his width, I pushed down until he hit the back of my throat, then quickly pulled back up. I hadn't gagged, but feeling my mouth so full of him was hard to adjust to. I started a slow pace up and down on his cock, making sure to lick the tip or underside each time I was back up. Once I built up a tolerance and rhythm, I increased my speed and made sure to hollow out my cheeks.

His enjoyment was evident when his hand tightened in my hair. His groans grew louder. Each time I felt him hit the back of my throat, he'd hold me there for a moment. He began to thrust his hips so I no longer had to move my head. Instead, he was lightly fucking my face, and I felt delirious with need at that point. The need to please him. The need to relieve myself, too.

"I'm going to fucking come, Hannah. That's how good you make me feel. If you don't want it in your mouth, pull away now," he advised. I wasn't a quitter. I wanted the full experience.

I pushed my mouth down until he was at the back of my throat, and I took his balls in my hand, playing with them for a few seconds before he released into my mouth with loud moans. Men moaning was sexy as fuck, and I hated that porn taught them that it wasn't normal. All I wanted was to hear Wyatt moan every night.

"Fuck, that's a good girl," he said. His cum just finished shooting down my throat, and I swallowed it. I sat back on my ass, wiping my mouth with my arm.

"Tastes so good," I said, winking at him. His eyes went wild.

"I want to be buried inside you so fucking bad right now," he said. I had never known Wyatt to swear so much, but an entirely different, more primal side of him came out when he was turned on. I liked it.

"So do it," I challenged, lifting my shirt - which was actually his - over my head and throwing it on the floor. I never imagined that giving someone a blow job would turn me on, but it did.

He pulled his boxers off and threw them near my shirt. He got off the bed, and I pouted, unsure of what he would do. He positioned himself at the edge of the bed, standing so he was facing me, his hips lined up with the height of the bed. Oh, now I knew where he was going with this.

"Come here," he demanded. He didn't need to tell me twice.

I positioned myself in front of him with my legs in the air, and he pulled down my panties so there were no more barriers between us. He wrapped my legs around his waist and leaned forward, coating his fingers in my arousal before shoving them inside of me, rough and quick. He needed to prepare me to take all of him, though no amount of fingering or lube could make him easy to take. His fingers curled inside of me, and I writhed beneath him until he removed his hand, smirking down at me.

CHAPTER THIRTY-ONE

"You know just where to touch me to make me feel good," I said.

"Good, because all I want to do is please you."

He leaned down to kiss me, his erection rubbing against my clit as he did. I kissed him back with passion. With his lips on mine, I reached between us and grabbed him, rubbing the tip along my folds a few times before pushing him inside of me. He broke our kiss to let out a groan.

"Fuuuck, Hannah," he said as he sank inside of me slowly. His movements started out slow and calculating. He'd thrust to the hilt, circle his hips, then pull away and do it all over again. He was slowly driving me crazy. I needed more.

Without speaking, he seemed to sense my need and began to thrust harder. I let out small moans, my fingers grabbing his shoulders and digging into the skin. The angle at which he hit me drove me wild.

"Yes, Wyatt, yes, that feels so good," I moaned. I might have been inexperienced, but Wyatt knew exactly what he was doing, and I was thankful for that.

"You take me so fucking well," he said with a rasp. His eyes darkened as he watched where we were joined, seeing himself slam in and out of me in rough, deep thrusts. "I'll never get enough of you." That was fine by me.

Wyatt leaned forward and took my nipple in his mouth. He licked, bit, and sucked the tiny bud in a rotation. Simultaneously, he reached between our bodies, his fingers finding my clit instantly like he had a gift. He pressed roughly in a side-to-side motion before switching to circles. The sensations all at once made me feel like I would pass out.

"I want you to come for me. I want to feel you come all over my cock and scream my name," he demanded.

With stars in my vision, my thighs started to shake, my body trying to move while being pinned to the bed by him. He sucked my nipple again as my moans turned into small screams, and my orgasm wildly burst through me while I screamed his name as he requested. Not because he told me to, but because I couldn't help it. He felt so good.

"Good girl, Hannah," he said.

He stilled inside me, and I felt his cock swell as he came, his groans turning into moans.

I was exhausted when he pulled out of me and laid himself on the bed.

"I'm going to clean up, then we can go back to cuddling," I said. Before I could stand, Wyatt got up from the bed and brought me a towel. The king of aftercare was at it again.

While I cleaned myself, he went into the bathroom and cared for his needs. Then, we changed into fresh clothes and returned to the same cuddling position.

"So, tomorrow is the big day. What time are we leaving? Can't wait to hit that ocean," Wyatt said excitedly.

"We have to drive two hours away, and I rented a car tomorrow that we have to pick up at nine. Our appointment is from noon until four, then we'll have to return the car around six thirty," I answered, explaining tomorrow's plans. Several days ago, I told him what I intended to do but never told him that plans changed. I planned a surprise for him. One that I know he'll enjoy.

"Sounds great. I'll probably fall asleep soon. I could sleep like this, with you in my arms," he whispered, his hand playing with my hair and causing me to smile against his chest.

"Me too," I said honestly, shocking myself.

Chapter Thirty-Two

Wyatt

Hannah suspiciously kept the details to a minimum as we drove a few hours away to swim with dolphins. Instead, she turned up her music when I asked her a question. She was blaring Taylor Swift and singing along. Currently, Vigilante Shit was blaring through the speakers. As an avid Taylor fan, I knew the song. I made a mental note to myself about her love so I could potentially surprise her with tickets one day, along with all of the information I stored in my brain about Hannah facts.

I could tell we were close when the ocean came into view, and for the last thirty minutes, we drove along the coast. It was incredible. I had seen it so few times, only with her, but I could see why she loved the ocean and beaches. We had a few beaches and a large body of water in Chicago, but Lake Michigan couldn't compare to the ocean, and the sand in Illinois didn't compare to the white Florida sand.

"It's so beautiful," she remarked, watching the coast as she drove. She wouldn't let me drive since she said she knew where we needed to be. I knew she was up to something, I just couldn't imagine what.

"Yes, it is," I responded, but she didn't notice I was looking at her. I watched her dance to the music, her hair swaying with the air coming from her rolled-down window. She was a beautiful sight.

She wore a one-piece black bathing suit with a pair of jean shorts over it, so it looked like she was wearing a tucked-in shirt. She said we needed to have easy access to our bathing suits for the dive. I went with my blue swim trunks with pink flowers, and a simple white polo shirt. I was sure that swimming with dolphins would be my second favorite activity in Florida, next to the night after the beach. Being with Hannah for the first time was better than I could have ever imagined.

When we pulled up into our parking spot and walked to the small shack on the beach, I was shocked that it was labeled Shark Diving.

I turned to Hannah, perplexed. My eyebrows cocked. "Shark diving? I don't see anything about dolphins." She grinned with pride.

"I got the idea when you mentioned sharks being incredible creatures. I did some research. Then, I bought out the shark diving experience for the day so we could do this alone. I wanted to surprise you because I wanted to do something for you, for once," she explained.

A response was stuck in my throat as my brain tried to comprehend Hannah being able to pull one over on me and surprise me. It wasn't like I thought she was too selfish to do something like this. I just didn't exactly expect it. She wanted to swim with dolphins, and she already booked the experience.

"I swam with dolphins once before, and it was fantastic, but this trip isn't just about me. It's about you, too. And you've convinced me to give sharks a try."

Without thinking anymore, I stopped walking and spun her around, pulling her body against mine and bringing her in for a small kiss. My palm was on her cheek as we kissed slowly a few times before pulling away. Her cheeks were a deep shade of pink, and she was biting her lip.

"What was that for?" she asked. I hoped kissing her in public wasn't too much for her. It was one thing to have sex in private when no one sees, but people were around us when I just kissed her. And I was still sorting through my feelings over everything that happened on vacation so far. I never dreamt that I'd get so close to getting the girl, and now I was scared to fuck it up a second time.

"For being incredible and giving up your experience to do something for me. You have always deserved more than Brad."

"I'm hoping that I can deserve you," she said quietly before turning around and walking inside the business. I wanted to tell her that she more than deserved me. That I questioned if I even deserved her. Instead, she had already made it inside and wasn't alone anymore. A worker was standing behind the counter.

"Hello! Hello!" a man said excitedly, walking out from behind the counter. "You must be Hannah and Wyatt, the newlyweds."

"That's us," I confirmed. Hannah took my hand in hers and squeezed when she heard my response. I could see the smile planted on her face with my peripheral vision. She didn't need to mention that we were newlyweds. We were far from the hotel and no one here would know us. It meant something to me that she wanted to keep up the ruse even when she didn't need to.

"Alright. I got some documents for you to sign, then we'll take you out. I'll be your guide, and Frank will be the captain." He gave us each a copy of our waiver to sign, and when we were done, we walked out back. We got on a small boat with him and the captain, and they loaded some gear on and handed it to us.

When the boat took off, he started to explain the safety procedures, and my nerves grew as we went further out into the ocean, and the shore faded into the background.

"You'll each wear a wet shirt, flippers, goggles, and a snorkel." He handed us a gear pile each, including the items he mentioned. Hannah removed her shorts before changing into her new outfit, leaving the goggles and snorkel off. I removed my shirt and replaced it with the one he gave me.

We arrived a few minutes later after he gave us a more in-depth description of our experience. Then, we anchored somewhere that seemed quite deep and terrifying. I liked sharks but wasn't a huge fan of open water when it was deeper than I was tall. Ironic considering I forced Hannah into the water.

Our guide cut up a few pieces of fish and threw them in the water, and minutes later, we could see sharks swimming nearby.

"Magnificent creatures," our guide said. He hooked us each up to a long rope that connected to the boat so we didn't stray from the area. Then, following his guidelines, we went into the water together. While hanging onto the rope, our snorkel was out of the water for breathing, and we looked below from the top, watching as the sharks gathered. They were stunning. There were a few different kinds. He told us that most were bull sharks, which were the most common that we'd see. We were allowed to touch any that came close, but since we were near the surface, none of them came up to us. Our guide, however, didn't stay on our rope. He jumped in with full diving gear and got to go further down than us. We watched from the surface as he petted sharks on top of their body, and they just let him before carrying on.

I grew up afraid of sharks, but I realized how incredible they were when I started to learn more in high school. Unlike popular belief, shark attacks were incredibly rare, and they didn't just wait around for humans to eat. Hannah still had some apprehension it seemed like, but she stayed with me and even held my hand.

The rope extended roughly one hundred feet away from the boat. Once we were as far out as we could go, sharks started to get more curious and come closer. I was in front of Hannah, and one went right past me. When it came up, I reached out my hand, and the back of the shark briefly rubbed against my hand. It was a magical experience that I had Hannah to thank for.

We spent a while down there, but I didn't know how long it was without my phone. He signaled us to head back, and we let the rope lead us back to the ship with ease.

"How was it?" Frank asked once we removed our face gear.

"Incredible," I answered.

"A little terrifying, but spectacular. I wouldn't have changed this event for anything else we could've done today," Hannah responded.

"You two will certainly remember your honeymoon forever."

Hannah took out her phone which she hadn't yet touched today, and made videos of the sharks that we could visibly see swimming nearby.

"My followers will eat this up," she said.

"Yeah, like the shark ate those fish," our guide said. The nametag he wore earlier said Alex, but I realized he never actually introduced himself, only Frank.

"I don't think I'll ever beat this experience," I said honestly.

"Let's get a picture of all of us!" Hannah beamed. I stood by Hannah's side as she extended her arm to take a group photo of us. Frank and the guide joined us, and we all smiled for a photo.

"Your experience does include lunch on the boat," Frank said.

Our guide brought out two coolers of food that we watched him grab earlier. Packed inside were cut fruits and vegetables and mini sandwiches. Hannah mentioned that she made the choices for us beforehand and picked out ham and swiss for me. I had never eaten a sandwich in front of her, but she got the choice right. We ate while anchored in the diving spot, and when we were done, we returned. We arrived at the shore a little early, which was good since we had a car to return.

"Thank you so much, Alex and Frank," Hannah said before we left. So his name was Alex.

"It was lovely to meet you, young lady. May you have many happy years of marriage," Frank said. She blushed when he mentioned our marriage.

I offered to drive the car back, and she let me. I let her play the music and kept my hand on her thigh as I drove. Occasionally, we'd look at each other, lock eyes, and smile. When we returned to the hotel, I knew exactly what I wanted to do.

Chapter Thirty-Three

Hannah

"This is your honeymoon that I crashed, so thank you so much for including me in your thoughts," Wyatt said as we entered our hotel for the evening. We agreed to order delivery or room service when we returned since we were exhausted from driving for hours and being out in the warm sun on a boat.

"I travel for a living. I don't remember you traveling at all. You need a real vacation more than I do, and it's technically not my honeymoon… since I didn't get married," I reminded him, but it was with a smile this time. Not a sad thought behind the statement.

When we reached the room, things changed drastically and unexpectedly. I went to ask Wyatt about dinner, but before I could, he had me pressed against the wall in a deep kiss. One hand gripped my hip while the other rested next to my head. The lower half of his body pressed into mine, and I let out a groan.

"I thought I'd show you how thankful I am," he said in a deep-toned whisper that sent shivers down my spine. I fisted the material of his shirt and pulled him closer to me, bringing our lips together again. His tongue ran along the seam of my lips, and I parted my mouth to let it in. Our tongues mingled for a moment before we went back to kisses that progressively got harder and more frantic. When he pulled away, I was out of breath.

"I'd love it if you kept showing me just how thankful you are," I said. I looked up at him with a smile, and he knew what I meant. Placing his hands under both of my thighs, he lifted me, and I wrapped my legs around him. He leaned in again, but this time his mouth trailed kisses from my jaw to my collarbone. I let out soft, quiet moans in response.

"You're insatiable, Hannah DeLayne," he said against my skin before pulling down the straps of my swimsuit and exposing my breasts. His mouth connected with my nipple, licking, sucking, and biting the tiny bud while I threw my head back against the wall. My hips bucked up to his in response, seeking friction.

"Only with you, Wyatt Maverick."

Hearing me say those words set him off, and he made me wrap my arms around his shoulders before he moved us to the bed, tossing me in the middle of the heart before climbing on top of me.

"Fuck me, Wyatt," I requested, hoping I sounded as seductive as I was attempting to.

He sat up while he removed the swimsuit the rest of the way from my body, taking my shorts with it. I lifted my hips to help him. He then took his shirt off, throwing it to the side. I looked up at him, drinking in the beautiful sight. I ran my hands along his chest, then hooked my fingers in the hem of his shorts, tugging them down. He took them off entirely, and then we were naked together. My back was on the bed, and he positioned himself to sit between my legs.

I was already wet from kissing him, but he still took the time for foreplay with me. His finger brushed against my clit a few times before he inserted two fingers inside of me.

"Jesus, Hannah, you're so wet for me already," he said with a groan.

"Kissing you will do that to a girl," I responded.

He thrust his fingers inside me a few times, curling them to hit my G-spot before withdrawing them. My moans ceased, and my eyes widened when he put the two fingers in his mouth, slowly sucking the juices from them.

"Good. Because now you're ready for me. And it's so fucking hot to see you want me the same way that I want you."

I leaned down between us and took his length in my hand. He was rock hard, and I ran my hand up and down his length, giving a gentle squeeze a few times. His eyes closed as he let out a few moans.

"And now you're ready for me," I responded.

With my hand free, he pressed his lower body against me, kissing me deeply a few times while his erection lay at my thighs. Then, when he pulled away, he lined himself up with my entrance and watched as he pushed inside of me in one swift motion. I shifted in the bed, letting out a moan as he filled me beautifully. We fit so perfectly together.

"You are so beautiful," he said before thrusting inside of me again. "So perfect for me." He started to build a steady pace.

The way he sat between me and placed my legs on his shoulders sent him deep inside of me, deeper than I had felt before. The sensation was incredible, but he made it more intense when he reached between us and began rubbing my clit. My body began to wither below his, making him smirk and thrust harder into me.

"Fuck, yes, Wyatt," I moaned. Since my legs were wrapped around his neck, I reached to my sides and grabbed his thighs with my nails while he pounded into me, deeply but slowly. I squeezed, my nails digging into his thighs while my moans grew louder. His breathing increased, and his groans became moans while I scratched down his leg.

"I want you to come for me," he said while increasing the pressure on my clit. His words helped the pressure build low in my body, and it quickly grew in intensity with his touch. My body always wanted to please his commands. He increased his pace and kept his depth, and it took only seconds to send me off the edge. I orgasmed with a small scream, and he stilled inside me while I did, burying himself deep as I contracted around him. "That feels so fucking good, Hannah."

"You feel so good, Wyatt," I responded.

He buried his face in my neck, and he bit on my skin, sucking enough to leave a hickey as he released inside of me. He was right. I was insatiable because I'd never get enough of Wyatt.

"Stay right here," he said as he pulled out of me, my legs dropping to the bed. I didn't move a muscle while my heavy breathing attempted to regulate itself. He came back a moment later with a wet washcloth. Unexpectedly, he parted my legs, using the washcloth to clean up the mess we had made on my body. The warm sensation felt comforting from the pain he created with his brutal thrusts. Wyatt was big, and it wasn't like I was incredibly experienced.

"Does that feel good for you?" he asked.

I nodded my head, and he smiled in return. He put the washcloth back in the bathroom. Then when he returned, he brought me water from the mini-fridge. After I drank some water, he gathered one of his shirts and a pair of my underwear and brought them to me, setting them down on the bed at my side.

"Lift your hips," he instructed, and he put on my panties for me. Then, I sat up, and he put on my shirt.

"You didn't have to do all of this. You do so much for me."

"Because it's you. I'd do anything for you, Hannah."

He put on his clothes and joined me in the bed. He handed me the room service menu.

"What are you thinking about getting?" he asked.

"Macaroni and a loaded potato. Don't judge," I answered honestly. He laughed.

"I'd never. In fact, I think I'm going to order a burger and fries. Keeping it simple myself."

The room service took twenty minutes after we ordered, and I didn't have to leave the bed. Wyatt brought the tray of food to me, setting it down in front of me. Our food looked good and was surprisingly warm and fresh despite having to travel here from the kitchen.

I never thought I'd enjoy sitting in a hotel room bed and eating room service so much, but with Wyatt, I could enjoy anything. He'd make every moment fun, and I loved that about him.

"Tell me something about you that no one else knows," I told Wyatt.

"I organize everything in my home by color, including the spines of my books and my underwear." I couldn't help but laugh. "Your turn."

"My mom died before Brad and I got engaged. I never told him because I had become so detached from her, but also because he treated her like she was garbage. I spent years knowing she'd die – she lost herself to drugs early on in my adult life. I had so long to prepare. I wasn't living with her for a long time, anyway." I hoped I didn't sound too much like a bitch when I talked about her.

"I knew she died, Hannah. Something was off about you that week, and you took off that necklace you wore all of the time. I found her obituary in the trash, then hid it from Brad, figuring you threw it away for a reason. It was why I brought flowers home that week and lied and said they were a kitchen decoration," Wyatt admitted. I didn't think he could say anything else that would shock me, but he did. He continued to reveal little truths that meant something bigger to me.

"I...never knew. Or I would have thanked you before. But thank you, seriously. I loved the smell of the flowers, and you couldn't have known, but they were her favorite. I smiled when I looked at them."

"There's nothing I wouldn't do to make you smile, Hannah."

After eating and relaxing for a few hours, we fell asleep cuddling together. A way of sleep I never thought I'd follow, but it was comfortable in his arms, and I knew in a few days I'd have to go back to sleeping alone, without his warmth.

Chapter Thirty-Four

Wyatt

I woke up before Hannah. My arms were wrapped around her, and she was facing me. I smiled at how cute she was when she slept. She drooled onto her hand under her palm, and I still thought she was adorable. I liked to watch her sleep peacefully, not just because she was cute, but because I didn't want to wake her up. If I moved from our position, she'd wake up, and then she wouldn't be in my arms anymore.

I never imagined coming to Florida would end up this way, but I was beyond happy that it did. I intended to hold off with Hannah, but she begged me for sex, and I couldn't resist. Her begging shocked me and made me extremely happy. I would give her anything she asked to hear her beg again.

I could tell she was waking up when she shifted beneath my arms and groaned. She blinked a few times before her eyes fully opened, and she smiled at me. "Good morning," she said.

I leaned down and kissed her cheek. "A very good morning indeed," I responded.

Tonight was our second-to-last day in Florida. With no idea what the future held, I wasn't ready for the trip to end. Soon, she'd be face-to-face with Brad again, and I'd return to being a full-time doctor. We'd leave our well-built bubble and see if our relationship could survive the real world if she even wanted that. She made it clear we were a vacation fling, but the way she looked at me, I felt she wanted more. I held no expectation of her, though, seeing as she was only recently single – and recently hurt.

"What does the day hold for us?" I asked.

She shrugged her shoulders, then escaped the grasp of my arm to sit up on the bed while I remained lying. She grabbed her laptop and set it on the bed, opening it and looking at something I couldn't see.

"I'm going to finish my article today, then I'm going to shower, and we'll talk about what to do. I have nothing else planned for the trip. Nothing booked."

"I'll go shower now," I offered.

I let her write, and I went to go shower. I turned the water to warm, then shut the door and turned on the fan, stripping to nothing. With my phone in the bathroom, I chose to look at things to do in the area. I wanted to surprise her.

Shit, of course. Disney World. Why hadn't I thought of that? We were in the city of Disney. Brad hated roller coasters, so she probably didn't plan to go. On the other hand, I loved the adrenaline rush they provided and the other attractions, too. I knew Hannah liked Disney movies and wanted to go to Disney World, but she constantly put everyone's needs above hers. She didn't go to Disney for her blog because she thought it would be too overdone and not offer her anything, but this Hannah now was different than the girl that said that.

I hopped in the shower and took the time to get clean. I used Hannah's shampoo since she reamed me out for my choices in hygiene products, and I loved the idea of smelling like her. She smelled like sunshine and flowers, somehow. Now, my hair did, too.

After putting on my clothes for the day, styling my hair, and brushing my teeth, I left the bathroom. When I entered the main room again, Hannah slammed her laptop shut and smiled at me.

"My turn, I guess." She left her laptop on the bed and jumped up, grabbing her clothes and bringing them into the bathroom. I heard the water running just seconds later.

I decided to pack all of my things while she showered since I didn't need much else beyond an outfit tomorrow that I could rummage for in the morning. I liked to remain organized to make things easy; Hannah was a little chaotic. Her clothes were spread out near her bag, while mine remained in drawers. Her makeup took over the bathroom counter the entire trip, despite her wearing less.

She was still in the shower when I finished. I knew it was wrong, but I had the urge to open her laptop and see what made her close it quickly. If she hadn't done that, I wouldn't be interested. I thought having a passcode on her laptop would stop me, but when I flipped it open, she didn't have one set. Instead, it opened up to the page she was writing on. I was horrified by what I found. A blog post in the making, talking about our time together on vacation. How we fucked, how we kissed. She sold the idea of fooling around with her fiance's brother like I was entertainment. She even outright admitted the truth about who I was. I felt the bile rise in my throat.

I sat there and read the entire thing before she was even out of the bathroom. I read it as I listened to her blow-drying her hair.

Eventually, she was done in the bathroom and walked in on me looking at her laptop. I stopped reading it, but I couldn't stop staring at it.

"Wait, I can explain," she said. "I wrote it, yes, but I didn't post it. I've been posting about the food, swimming, and beach, but I didn't post this. It's just a draft." She tried to justify what she had written, but I couldn't see past my anger at the moment.

I got up from the bed and set her laptop down, pacing around the bed and thinking. She used me for content. Our entire vacation fling was nothing to her but a means to more views.

"I...I need a break," I told her. I took a hotel key, my wallet, and my phone and walked out of the room in a fury. I needed time to process what I read and think about it while thinking about everything that happened this past week.

I was seething when I left our room. Sure, Hannah hadn't posted it, but she still wrote it down with the intention of sharing our story. It would be one thing if it were a story about how she realized she fell in love with me, but it was just a story for her followers to bring attention to her blog. And it would. I couldn't believe I let her reduce me to a story, someone she used to write about for attention. It hurt.

But, the longer I sat in the lobby gathering my thoughts, the more I thought about how I knew she was lying. Maybe she was trying to drive me away. Sure, the article was real and way too detailed, but she didn't post it. Instead, she posted boring stuff about our trip, though she didn't mention me. Not the real me, anyway.

I decided to head back up. I spent an hour down here after finding out the truth on her laptop, and I was going to finally lay it all out on the table and tell her how I felt. I could forgive her for this. I knew Hannah more than she thought, and I knew she wouldn't use me to gain attention herself. She wanted me; she just didn't want to admit it. Earlier, she said she needed to tell me something tonight.

When the elevator opened, my heart sank. Our room was close, and I heard a male's voice. Not just any man's voice, but my brother's obnoxious voice begging for another chance.

"I'm beyond sorry, Hannah. I love you, and I know I don't deserve a second shot," he said. It was quiet after that, except for the noise of their lips together. I moved closer towards the voices, peeking out of the hallway, and he had her pressed against the wall with his hand near her head. More importantly, their lips were touching.

"Sorry to intrude," I said as I stepped closer to the door they stood next to.

"Fuck," Hannah said, shoving Brad away.

That was what she wanted, to end things between us. To tell me that she was forgiving Brad and giving him another chance. Soon, she'd be my sister-in-law. One with which I slept.

In a rush, I ran into the room, grabbed my packed suitcase, and flew out the door. I didn't want to see her, and I especially didn't want to see them together. It made me sick.

Deep down, I knew I was just a relationship fling to try to get over him. I failed. I failed. I liked to think I knew her better than most, but I was just her future brother-in-law who watched her too closely when they lived together. Knowing how she liked her coffee didn't mean I knew what type of person she was. Somehow, I once again failed to measure up to Brad, the cheating accountant.

When I exited the hotel room, she was standing there, Brad barely behind her.

"Wyatt, wait," she demanded, sticking her arms out in front of her to stop me from moving. "Brad kissed me. I didn't ask him to. I didn't want him to. Please, believe me," she pleaded.

I looked behind her, towards Brad, and he had a smirk on his face. A smirk that quickly diminished when he processed that Hannah and I had something going on while here. Or else she wouldn't be trying to get me to listen to her and deny she wanted to kiss him.

"My brother and my fiancé?" Brad said, looking between us. "Did you fuck him, Hannah?"

I let out a chuckle for some reason, answering his question.

"Absolutely not. My Hannah would never. I was her first, her only, and her last." Brad struggled with the thought of us together.

"I'm not your Hannah, and we're not engaged anymore. You cheated on me, and you got another girl pregnant. And she was a friend."

"You hated her. You just lied to yourself to pretend she was a friend, so you could feel more betrayed. If you like to fuck liars, Hannah, then you should just come back to me. Nicole was lying, thanks to my mother," Brad explained. I rolled my eyes. I refused to believe anything he said in an attempt to get what he wanted. He was used to being the spoiled kid growing up, and his entitlement never ended.

"I'm not interested in liars, Brad. Especially not cheaters, either."

I shook my head when Brad looked towards me, knowing what he was about to say. I silently pleaded with my brother, but why would he listen? He wanted her, and she didn't want him, but at least he could ruin things between us. She'd never forgive me.

"That's funny because you screwed my brother, and I doubt he told you that he knew about Nicole and me since before we were engaged," Brad said with a devious smirk on his lips.

Hannah's eyes stared at me, sharp like daggers. She was trying to read me, waiting for an answer. Waiting for me to say it wasn't true, but it was. That was what she heard me tell Brad, that he needed to end things with Nicole, not her. Hannah deserved faithfulness, even if it wasn't from me. From me, though, she deserved honesty. Especially if I told her I had been in love with her for years. How can you lie to someone and claim to love them?

"What was this, Wyatt? What are we doing here? Fucking me out of pity, or are you just trying to claim what your brother had?"

"You tell me, Hannah. What was this? You trying to get material for your blog at the expense of me, or were you fucking me to get back at my brother?"

I felt the sting of her hand hitting my cheek. I admit I might have deserved that.

"Get the fuck out of here, both of you," she seethed. When we didn't move for a few seconds, she raised her voice, adding, "NOW!"

I took my suitcase and walked down the hall and back towards the elevator, not even caring if I left anything behind. Brad was right next to me, but the walk back was silent. When we entered the elevator, he said, "We really fucked that up."

"I know," I agreed. Brad was the one that fucked everything up, but my blind rage and secrets ruined things, too. All Hannah wanted was someone to be honest with her, and I couldn't even do that.

Chapter Thirty-Five

Hannah

I thought about chasing after Wyatt and apologizing. I regretted the things I said. Unlike Brad, I knew he cared about me and wanted me for me. I knew he was an honest man, and he deserved an explanation. I would've been mad if I walked in on him being kissed by someone else and didn't even explain that I wasn't kissing him back. I was about to slap him before I was made aware of Wyatt's presence. It looked terrible, and I reacted poorly.

I had one more night in Florida, and now I was on my own. I needed a break anyway, so it was a good thing. I hadn't been alone for a while and jumped right from Brad to Wyatt without time alone. After today, I'd have quite a lot of time alone, and now I knew the trip was perfect for me. I needed to get away from Chicago.

I heard a knock on the door a little after they left and figured it was one of them coming back for me. My heart thudded before I listened to the voice on the other end. Priya. I didn't know how she was standing outside my hotel room, but I was thankful she was. I sped my way to the door, opening it to my best friend, and she enthusiastically jumped in my arms.

"What are you doing here?" I asked, clinging to her.

"I knew Brad was coming here, and I knew it would end in a shit show, so I left shortly after I found out he was on his way. I kind of…am why he came here. He found out you were here by sending Nicole to snoop; I'm so sorry. Where's Wyatt?" Priya looked around, noticing he and his suitcase were missing.

"He left. Or, rather, I told him to go. He said some mean stuff, I said some mean stuff, it was a whole thing," I explained.

"Are you going to go after him?"

"No. It's best this way. I'm going to head home tomorrow, spend a few days packing all of my stuff and moving it, and then leave the country. It's good that you're here, though. I needed to ask you something."

"Go for it," she said, letting me go and closing the door behind us. She took a seat on the bed before laying back on it and sprawling out. "Wow, this is comfortable. So you've been sharing this with Wyatt, eh? On second thought, maybe I shouldn't lay here."

I laughed. "I have realized on this trip that I want more time to live through my adventures and less time focusing on the business aspects. I want to take you on full-time, bring you with me on my trips, and have you help me create content. If you're interested," I offered.

Priya jumped with joy. "Yes! I've been waiting for you to bring me on full-time for years now. And pay me more for my work," she said with a tease.

"I should have brought you from the beginning. You're my best friend, and it'll be that much more fun with you joining me."

"Let's go get drunk to celebrate my new job and wallow in your relationship misery," Priya suggested with a laugh. I needed her brutally honest humor to get me through my feelings. She understood me.

"You know exactly what I need," I told her.

"Yeah, and right now, you need a little makeover. What even is this outfit? Hannah doesn't wear jean shorts. Get a sundress on now, and put on some lipstick," she demanded. This was why Priya was my other half. I didn't need shitty men when I had her by my side. My favorite person on this planet. How many people had a best friend that would fly out of state to be there for them at the last minute?

As long as I was distracted by her, I wouldn't cry. I wouldn't think about how I just sent my fiancé away for the second time or how I slept with his brother days after our wedding was supposed to happen, only for him to be an accusatory asshole in the end and ruin our trip.

I wouldn't think about how I let another Maverick brother in, only to end up with a broken heart in the end.

I followed Priya's suggestion and put on a cute sunflower dress that I was planning to wear on a date with Wyatt tonight, but now it would be a date with Priya. It was moments like this that made me happy I sprung for eyelash extensions. It made simple makeup look easier. Within fifteen minutes, I was ready to go with red lips, a cute dress, and just enough concealer to even out my skin tone.

Tonight, I planned to have a serious discussion with Wyatt about how things would be when we got home. I was going to lay it all on the table, tell him how I felt and everything. I told him I only wanted a quick vacation fling, but I realized that wasn't true. I was simply scared to let someone in again, only to get hurt.

Thinking back, I realized that my feelings for Wyatt developed over time. I thought I was just intrigued by him because he perplexed me with his blind hatred of me, but really, I just wanted to feel good enough for him. He piqued my interest. We were alike, definitely more than Brad and I. I didn't have to face any potential feelings until we kissed the night of my bachelorette party. I knew it was him, and I still didn't stop immediately. I convinced myself it was because I had been drinking, but it was years of pining culminating at once. It was the connection of our souls

"You look amazing, babe. Let's go get fucking blasted," she said, smacking my ass on the way out the door. I missed my best friend. And now I wouldn't have to travel without her.

One ten-minute Uber ride later, and we were at a random bar she found on Yelp. I told her I wanted cheaper drinks, good food, and somewhere without a dress code, and we ended up at this dive bar on karaoke night. I knew I'd regret it later, but it didn't make it any less exciting. Where I lived, these bars were hard to come by. The beers we ordered were five dollars cheaper than the ones I had the night I went out with Melissa and Adam. Wyatt and I spent so much time living the high life here, I needed something to bring me back down to earth.

"Want to split some fried pickles and fries?" Priya questioned, chugging down her beer after she set down the menu.

"What a way to celebrate our new partnership, but yes, of course." I was reminded of the simple things I enjoyed when we went out together. Sometimes we'd go to a fancy restaurant, eat meals that cost so much despite serving so little and drink expensive bottles of wine, but we'd often just enjoy bar grub. On this trip, it was brought to my attention that my usual way of living was pretentious, so I enjoyed this moment even more and showed Priya how I was still me.

When our waiter came back, Priya ordered us the food. "So what's the plan in Scotland?"

"I'm not sure. I didn't get asked to go there or anything. I just want to do this just for me. I want to do a series of day-to-day life exploring. I have always wanted to go because it's beautiful in pictures, and I can't believe I haven't been there yet." I found myself smiling just thinking about it. It felt like my life was taking a new, exciting turn. "Before we go, I must make a video for my followers. The ones that support me will still be there, but I might lose some."

"The ones worth keeping will stick around. Unless you, like, murdered a dog, or something, then they wouldn't. Neither would I."

The waiter dropped off our food, and I ordered us a shot of rum, each with a chaser of Coke. I wanted to have a fun time, but I wanted to remember it, too. One beer and one shot seemed like enough to help me let loose.

"Okay, I'm challenging you tonight," Priya said as she downed her shot faster than me. "No phone, no guys, just be here with me."

I brought my phone out of my purse and turned it off before putting it back. "Just us."

We sat in silence while we ate the food, and it was delicious. Better than any fifty-dollar entree I had bought in the last several years, surprisingly. "I can't believe I'm leaving Florida tomorrow afternoon right after we found this place. I haven't had fried food that tasted so good in such a long time."

"I can't believe I'm in Florida. I actually quit my job to come out here. I felt like you'd need me, and I didn't want to risk not being there if you did."

I was thankful that the next chapter of my life would be traveling the world with my best friend. I felt bad that I didn't involve her earlier, but now I realized that everything I wanted Brad to be, Priya already was. I didn't need him. I didn't need Wyatt. I only needed us.

"I won't blame you if you meet a hot Spanish man and fall in love on our travels, by the way. Don't let me hold you back," I told her. She said I didn't need a man, but I needed her to know that while she didn't either, it was welcomed. I supported her.

"I wouldn't blame you either. Maybe we'll find, like, a set of twins or some best friends. Or a hot father and son duo."

I cringed. I wasn't sure if Priya wanted the father or the son, but I wanted neither. In fact, I didn't want to meet anyone at all.

"Or, I can settle for traveling with my best friend before I have to settle down eventually."

"Who says you have to give up traveling just because you meet someone?" she questioned.

I thought about it. I thought about how Brad wanted me to have a child immediately and stay home while he worked. The idea always gave me hives, but I accepted that being with him meant that one day my life would head in that direction.

"You're right. A true partner won't let me put aside my wants for their own. Maybe, they'll travel with me, and we'll build that life together." My smile turned into a frown at remembering who made me believe that. "Wyatt told me those words. He was right."

"I knew I never liked that motherfucker, Brad. He tried too hard to change you. Wyatt, on the other hand, I do like. I'm sorry. I know we hate him right now."

"Why didn't you tell me you didn't like Brad?" I questioned, blinking a few times. Priya was known for being brutally honest, but I didn't remember her saying anything negative about him.

"Babes, I tried, but you wouldn't hear it. You had heart emojis over your eyes. You grew up knowing little love, so when you found it with someone, you clung onto him even if he was bad for you. You're lucky that you didn't fall for his bullshit. You remained you, for the most part," she explained.

The waiter came back around to clear our tables, and I ordered a few cocktails for us. "I'm not drunk enough yet," I proclaimed. Priya grinned at me. She loved when I'd get plastered and let loose, and tonight she'd get that side of me again. I needed to drink until last week was erased from my memory.

"We're celebrating, and we're wallowing," Priya said, clinking our cocktails together before we started chugging.

"Misery loves company," I said.

"Good thing you're miserable, and I'm great company."

Chapter Thirty-Six

Hannah

When I woke up in the morning, Priya was still sound asleep. She was a heavy drinker, and she was wasted last night. At least three times more drunk than me, I'd say. It was ironic that we went out to cheer me up, but she ended up being the one to have all of the fun. She even sang karaoke, and I had never seen her sing before. It was hilarious enough that I recorded it to taunt her later.

I knew what I had to do before I prepared to board the plane back to reality. I also knew I had to tie up loose ends here before leaving, doing the right thing. I turned on my phone's camera and set it up with my desktop ring light. I prepared to address my fans with a straight-out-of-bed look, which felt like a brand-new sense of self.

"Hello, my lovely followers. Today is the day I'm heading home. I have absolutely loved my stay here at Summit Resort and Spa, and everything you've seen from the hotel was shot here. The rooms, the pool, the spa, the food, and the staff were all absolutely incredible. Unfortunately, my stay was built on a lie, one that I must rectify. The man in my videos was not my husband. I was supposed to marry Brad last week but found out he was cheating the day of the wedding. Instead, I brought his brother on our honeymoon on a whim. I thought we'd spend our trip separately, but we spent our time together. I should have been clear with

Brad before the honeymoon that I wasn't marrying him, and I should have been clear with the hotel that he wasn't my husband. We spent a week putting on a charade, one that brought us closer, but eventually, I realized it was all a facade anyway. I will pay the hotel for my entire stay for lying and technically failing my contractual duties, and I will return to this amazing establishment. I know I've lived a life of showcasing luxury and fun, which I do have and enjoy, but I also want to make time to be real and honest, like now. This is how I wake up—the same way as everyone else, with frizzy hair, bad breath, and smeared makeup. I plan to take a few days off to pack and set up my next adventure, but then I'll be back online when I get there. For now, it's a surprise."

Hitting the stop button was a huge relief. Usually, I'd schedule a later time to post the video to my social media profiles, but instead, I released it. Instead of posting it on my story, I made a direct post so it could be shared easily. Maybe I should have asked Priya first as the new head of my social media, but I needed to do this for myself, and I knew she'd approve of being my authentic self.

"Wake up, sleeping beauty, it's time to pack," I called out to Priya before throwing a pillow at her head.

"Fuck off," she said, burying herself under the pillow.

"I will be in like an hour, so you have to get up, too. When are you leaving, anyway?"

"My plane is late at night. I want to enjoy some time at Disney World while I'm here."

"You can't enjoy the magic of Disney from my hotel room bed, babe," I pointed out. She groaned before removing the pillow and coming to life. "I'll pack while you get ready, then we'll leave together and catch separate Ubers," I suggested. She nodded her head while heading into the bathroom, and I started picking up the clothes I had thrown on the floor, packing things more like Wyatt's system than the one I used, which was to place everything in the bag chaotically.

While I packed, Priya took a shower and changed her clothes for the day. I could hear my phone buzzing on the counter nonstop, but I avoided it for now. If people left rude comments, I didn't want to see it and ruin my day. When Priya exited the bathroom, she looked at the buzzing phone.

"Why is it going off so much? What'd you do?" she asked. Before I could answer, she grabbed the phone and opened it, seemingly reading the post. Since I posted it to a picture-sharing app, I included the picture of Wyatt and me and the shark-diving people to grab attention.

"Holy fuck, Hannah," Priya said. Her mouth was wide open, and I didn't know if it was good or bad. "He's a hottie. Keep him. Says some girl named Jessica, who has tens of thousands of likes as the top comment. I knew something was strange about you guys, but you're seriously perfect together. From Melissa, who the hell is that?"

"She's someone I met with Wyatt, and we spent some time together," I answered, sighing. "This whole thing is a shit show."

"It may be, but babes, this has more likes and engagement than any of your posts ever, and it's hardly been up for an hour." I could hear the excitement radiating from Priya's voice. "But Christ, you couldn't check with your new Social Media Manager yet?" she teased.

"Let's get going. Check-out is now, and I've got a plane to catch. Alone."

Priya followed behind me with her small bag as I went to check out, my heart racing as I approached the desk.

"Ah, Miss DeLayne. Are you checking out?" the employee said with a smile. I was about to ruin things, and hopefully, they didn't hate me.

"Yes, and I actually need to pay for my stay. I lied and didn't fulfill the terms of my contract," I admitted.

"As far as I'm concerned, you've garnered attention for the hotel that we couldn't buy. We've been bombarded with support. Everyone wants to stay at the hotel you stayed at and the place you loved. Seems fulfilling to me," she said.

"Wyatt was never my husband, and I feel bad about the lie we told. I can pay for my room. Just tell me your rate."

"Oh, well, it looks like it's been closed out just now. Nothing is due, and I can't go back." She said with a wink and a shrug.

"Thank you so much. If you need anything from me, don't hesitate to contact me. I loved my stay here, and it wasn't my intention to lie, though I did anyway. I'm so sorry."

I apologized and left with Priya, but the girl didn't stop smiling as I walked away. She clearly cared less about my actions than I did, but I couldn't help but feel guilty.

Chapter Thirty-Seven

Wyatt

"Brad is still your brother, Wyatt, and no girl can change that." My mother had spent the past few weeks trying to get me to forgive him. I would, eventually. For now, he was still the guy who ruined things between Hannah and me twice. All over petty jealousy and the need to have everything to himself, and leave nothing for me.

I agreed to visit Mother today when she told me he'd be out. He and Dad took the day off together to go golfing. Since our dad had been setting up a new office across the country, he hadn't been around for months. Mom didn't care to spend time with him, and I didn't have much in common with the man, unlike Brad. They enjoyed golfing and accounting and being rich, unfaithful men.

When I heard the front door close, I figured it was one of her many workers coming inside. She had a team of landscapers, a maid, a chef, a personal assistant for whatever reason, and more that I couldn't even remember. Then, I heard male voices of Brad and my father. I felt betrayed. Of course, it was a setup. My mother played me, and I fell into the trap.

Noticing my frustration and acknowledgment of what was about to happen, she put her arms out to stop me from moving and said, "Just give it a chance, Wyatt. Talk to him." Before I could run, he was in the kitchen, where we stood.

"Wyatt, what are you doing here? Mom, what is he doing here?" Brad asked like a spoiled teenager. He had no golf gear, but our dad was with him. Was he in on it? Where did they go together, if not golfing?

"It was a setup, genius. I don't want to see you more than you want to see me, and I don't want to forgive you."

"Forgive *me*? You went on my honeymoon with my fiancé, and you slept with her before she even told me it was over. Then, you lied to her and tried to hide her from me without giving her a choice." Brad's voice gradually raised the longer he spoke.

"You cheated on Hannah for over a year. She told you she was leaving with me. You really didn't get the hint that you were done? You held out hope; why? You knew I liked her years ago, and you still went for her," I pushed. My voice started to unintentionally raise. I never thought I'd yell at my brother, but he was on my last nerve. Always playing victim to stuff he did.

"Boys, stop this. You're brothers. No woman is worth fighting over. I love you boys, and you love each other," our mother interjected.

"Yeah, you love me so much that you'd pay a girl to pretend to be pregnant to ruin my relationship?" Brad's anger was directed at our mother instead of me this time. "You wouldn't just let your son be happy?" He had her there. Her plan wouldn't have worked on me, because I would've never cheated on Hannah. If I was the one with her, and not Brad, would she have even cared enough to do something like that?

"Yeah, Mom, what you did was kind of fucked up," I chimed in unprompted, earning a glare from her. I called her mother so much in my head that it felt weird to say the word mom out loud.

"No matter what I thought of you, beyond my idea of protecting you from her, you still didn't deserve her. I know what it's like to be cheated on for years, and I knew you didn't truly love her, Brad. You loved that I told you not to go for her and that she was beautiful. But you didn't love her, or else you wouldn't have cheated." After finishing her small speech, she looked over at our father, who, unsurprisingly, walked out of the room. It wasn't like they hid their past issues from us growing up. We knew what he did, and we knew our mom allowed it. She wanted to give us the best life possible and gave up her future for us long ago. Shortly after, she followed our father out of the room, leaving Brad and me alone in the kitchen.

Brad was the first to break the silence. "Mom's right. I think I started chasing Hannah because you liked her, and I wanted something you didn't have. Then, Mom hated her, and it made me want her more. Truthfully, we weren't a good match in the end since we didn't want the same things. She wants someone to travel with her, and I want her to quit work and raise a family. But you're a busy doctor who refuses to unload his workload, so if you want a chance with her, you can't be the same person you are now."

"I don't have a chance with her, either way. You made sure of that." There was a hint of anger in my voice, but I was beginning to feel bad for him. "And you wanted something I didn't have? You have dad's respect, the job you wanted, and growing up, we were both given everything we asked for."

"I followed his career path because he made me. He threatened to cut me off. You got to go to school and do what you wanted, and they still love you the same. Hannah does, too, if you couldn't tell by her blog post. That's why I'm so mad. We broke up a week ago, and she moved on from me so fast. Like our relationship was nothing to her."

"The only person who the relationship meant nothing to was you," I pointed out. "Wait – blog post?" I questioned. I forgot Hannah was releasing her blog post about the trip last week. I saw her video admitting the truth, and after they tracked me down, my blank

Instagram gained tens of thousands of followers. People on the internet were ruthlessly intent on what they wanted, given that Hannah hardly released any information about me, and my Instagram was only a few days old.

"Dude, come on. You expect me to believe you weren't stalking her page, waiting to see what she said, but I was? Lame."

Before our falling out, I had alerts set on all of her pages for when she posted. For now, I wanted to get her off my mind so I could start to move on. It was my own fault that I was hurt, and I didn't want to think about it. It felt like I lost her twice.

I hurried to the living room to get my phone that I had left on an end table, opening it up to her blog. There it was, a week ago. She hadn't posted since — at least not on her blog's website. I decided to read it to see what he was talking about. First, it was a recap of how I pretended to be her husband for a week and how she and Brad hadn't gone through with their wedding. She talked about how much she loved the trip, how much fun she had meeting Melissa and Adam, and about our time on the beach is one of her favorite memories. What really stood out to me was the ending.

I can sit here and tell you all day that the hotel, beach, dining, pool, and spa were amazing, but what I really need to talk about is how I unexpectedly fell in love with my fiance's brother. I thought he hated me, but the minute we landed, he became everything I needed. For a moment, I thought I needed a quick fling with a guy that hadn't been serious with a woman, but I quickly learned he wasn't serious about anyone because he had spent years wanting me. Each day, I learned something new about him, and my opinion of him shifted. But I mistakenly wrote a blog about how I was using him for sex to get over Brad, and he left. Except, he came back and caught Brad kissing me and trying to apologize. When Brad told me that Wyatt knew he had cheated on me previously, I flipped out and sent them both packing. I returned home, packed my things, and left. Now, I'm in Scotland, and it doesn't matter how I feel because I'm going to be here for a long time. He's in Chicago. I'm excited to share my new Spain adventures with you and thrilled that my best friend, Priya, will be joining us. Make sure when you find love to hold onto it close. Who knows, maybe I'll find love here.

Over my dead body. Hannah loved me, but instead of telling me, she ran away to Scotland. But if she wrote the blog, she must have known I'd eventually read it. It was her way of telling me how she felt. She was always better at sharing her feelings with the world than the source.

I did what I knew I had to do, and I picked up the phone, making a few calls that would change my life forever.

Chapter Thirty-Eight

Hannah

Flying home was terrifying. I wasn't sure if Brad would be at the condo, and I had only days to pack my things. During that time, I had to decide what I wanted to bring with me and what I wanted to leave behind. I'd give Brad the condo since I didn't have a use for it. All of my stuff was going into storage, except what I chose to pack.

I could've asked Brad to pick me up, and he would have, but instead, I chose to take a Taxi waiting outside the airport. It was a nerve-wracking drive from O'Hare to our lakeside condo. I hoped he wasn't there and that I could pack in peace. I hired movers tomorrow to bring everything I didn't want to storage. Truthfully, because of my travels, I didn't have much.

I sighed when I pulled up to the condo, wishing we lived in the suburbs so I could've looked to see if his car was there. It was quiet at first when my elevator opened in the condo. Within seconds, Brad appeared in a few. "Hannah?" he asked, a shocked look on his face.

"Hi, Brad," I said. Not wanting to give him the wrong message, I hurriedly walked past him, heading to our shared bedroom. I looked around, thinking about what I wanted to bring with me. I was starting an entirely new chapter of my life.

"You're back," he said plainly.

"For my things, Brad. Not for us," I pointed out, opening my closet and looking around. A week ago, I loved these clothes. Owning them made me feel important and special and reminded me of how far I had come from my past. Now, the clothes made me sick to look at. They weren't...me. Wyatt helped point that out.

"We can work on us, Han. I love you. Please. I messed up, but I won't again. I just had cold feet."

Anger rattled my bones at his excuses. I whipped around, closing the distance between us and pointing my finger at his chest. "*You* don't get to call me that name; only Priya can. You started fucking her before we were engaged, Brad. You shouldn't have proposed to me if you had cold feet that far out. I don't want you anymore." I hope I made myself clear this time.

"And you shouldn't have accepted my ring if you were going to be off traveling the world instead of starting a fucking family here with me. Did you even think how lonely you made me? We got engaged, and you started traveling more and more. We were supposed to be together."

"Maybe that's true, but you didn't have to step out. Your job was to work with me. Go to counseling. Travel more. Anything but stick your dick in a younger woman. Instead, you chose an easy way out, and now you want it both ways. You and I were never meant to be. In fact, you stole me from the man who could have given me everything I wanted." I was still bitter over the truth Wyatt revealed at dinner. Brad took credit for the book, but he knew all along where it had come from. I thought he was the stranger I ran into, but it was Wyatt all along.

He sighed, accepting defeat before starting to walk out the bedroom door.

"Brad," I said, catching his attention with hopeful eyes. "You can do whatever you want with what I leave here. I don't give a shit anymore. You're in the past, and I'm thinking about the future."

I shut my closet door, ready to leave my old clothes behind. They were everything Brad wanted me to be, but now I was becoming who I wanted to be. No more prissy, stuck-up girl. Whenever I tried to humble myself, Brad was in my ear, reminding me how I came from nothing, creating a bitter need to show off my worth constantly and become the kind of girl he wanted. The kind of girl he'd no longer have to remember where she came from.

I sighed with relief when I set that key on the counter and walked out the front door. Whatever I needed for now would be in my luggage bag that I still had. Whatever I needed after I moved, I'd buy. Minimalism was always more of my style.

Chapter Thirty-Nine

Hannah

The same day I packed all my things was the day I left the country. I went to Scotland on a solo trip. It was something I always wanted to do for myself. Once there, I posted my blog about my trip and my feelings for Wyatt. Then, I left my blog and social media accounts alone for a few days. Scotland was my transitional place. Priya had some things to finish back home before she moved to meet me in Spain, giving me a few days alone in Scotland. It was cold and gloomy but gorgeous. I visited a few places I had fallen in love with on my television screen, which showed me how stunning the country was.

Alnwick Castle was the first place on my list. With only a few days in Scotland, I knew I needed to hit a few major places and make choices. I spent most of my time exploring. The castle exceeded my expectations. It was stunning in person and brought me back to being a kid again and watching the Harry Potter movies for the first time.

I visited the Glenfinnan Viaduct to watch the train go by. Thankfully, someone local had told me when to catch it. It was just as gorgeous as I expected. Even the gloomy weather couldn't dull Scotland's shine.

I bought a disposable film camera at a store to take my pictures with. I wanted to leave my phone alone and have these memories just for myself. It felt weird at first, but it felt right.

A few days after arriving, I checked out of my hostel and headed to Spain. Just like I imagined, Spain was a dream. Needing a break from being around beaches, I first arrived in Madrid. Before returning to clear water and sand, I wanted to experience food and culture. I hadn't posted since I advertised my blog post, and I made ten grand from two ads on the website alone. They knew it would be my biggest post yet, and according to statistics, it was.

Priya joined me a day after I arrived, ready to start her new job. We spent a few days adjusting to our new rental, and so far, within six days, we created a few Instagram posts of local restaurants that we loved. Priya told me that we'd find a new one every day. We agreed to two weeks in Madrid and two weeks in Barcelona. After the month was complete, it was undecided where we'd go next. I was just happy she was by my side.

We even thought about doing a series where we picked out where we'd visit by an automatic generator or through a hat. It was genius, actually. Priya was a marketing genius.

"Have you heard from Wyatt yet?" she asked quietly, scared that saying his name would upset me. I poured my heart out online with hopes he would see it, but if he did, he didn't say anything to me yet. Maybe what we had was simply a vacation fling. I shook my head in response.

"Babe, to be fair, you didn't call him and tell him how you felt. You didn't even try to see him before you packed your life away and moved to another country." I hated it when she tried to make sense. Priya spent too many years in therapy and was too emotionally stable for me. She tried to rub that stability onto me.

"I really needed to get out of there. I wish I talked to Wyatt before scaring him off twice in one day. Maybe he gave up on me. It wasn't like I ever deserved him; maybe he finally realized that." A part of me did feel like I didn't deserve him. He wanted me, and I couldn't even remember when we met for the first time. Beyond that, I didn't chase him because while he helped me realize who I wanted to be, I didn't *need* him. I needed my best friend, and I needed to do something that would make me happy without a man. Moving did that for me.

If he showed up for me and confessed his feelings, I wouldn't turn him away. But I'd no longer be the desperate girl chasing after a man.

Priya sighed loudly. "You've got to stop talking about yourself like that, Han. You're everything a man could ever want. Remember that he wanted you first, and he wanted you all of those years. You are beautiful, smart, fun, chaotic, disorganized, kind, and caring. You let one man devalue you, and for that, I'm going to finally chop his dick off," Priya ranted angrily.

"Initially, I thought he loved me and always wanted the best for me. Now, I see he wanted to control me and do what was best for him. I just need to remind myself that every crack he made at me that ate away at my self-esteem was just a way of manipulating me and controlling me." I was amazed that I learned all that from reflecting on our relationship without attending therapy. It felt like something a therapist would tell me.

Priya and I arrived at our destination, a little Spanish restaurant a fifteen-minute walk from where we were staying. The architecture here was stunning, and this place was no different. The streets were clean, full of people walking, and beautifully lit in the evening, like now.

I ordered something called buñuelos de bacalao, and it was so incredible that I immediately took a few pictures for tonight's post. Our food series was a big hit, after all. Melissa commented recently that she wanted to travel to Spain because of me. I encouraged her to. I would love for Priya and Melissa to meet.

I thought Melissa would be mad after finding out the truth, but she was incredibly supportive. She told me she suspected all along, which was why she tried to push us together more. It worked, seeing as we first hooked up after she made us kiss at the beach.

"Your birthday is coming up, and I have a surprise planned," Priya said.

I groaned. "Just what I need, to grow another year older, alone," I grumbled. I didn't really care about being alone. I just cared that I lost relationships with two people I cared about within a few weeks. Meanwhile, it was Wyatt that hurt the most.

"Maybe we'll go clubbing and meet hot Spanish men." Priya shimmied her shoulders, and I shook my head at her, rolling her eyes.

"I can't take you anywhere, can I?" I joked.

"You should be taking me everywhere. Especially clubbing to meet hot men."

"As your boss, I'm going to need your focus to be on me and not men," I teased.

"Gosh, don't I get a break sometimes, or am I on the clock 24/7?" she questioned with a cocked brow and a fake curiosity.

"I suppose you're on the clock constantly since I pay you a salary. A decent one, if I do say so myself."

"I think tonight's dinner should be included in my benefits package," she said.

I laughed. "We can do that. But tomorrow, it's your turn to pick a place for us to eat at."

Chapter Forty

Hannah

When my birthday rolled around, Priya and I decided to head to Barcelona, where we had another rental set up. We decided to only rent places with furniture and never brought more than a large suitcase of items. My makeup collection had dwindled to eyeliner, mascara, lipstick, and concealer. My clothing collection had grown, but I folded them in a way that fit all of my outfits in one suitcase.

By now, my travel account was focused less on staying at fancy hotels and more on food and fun in new places. I enjoyed making the content I always wanted to, but I had yet to think I would. I let the followers and dollar signs get to my head and instead took deals that would get me to new places for free. Now, not only did I go where I wanted, but I lowered the monthly sponsorships I chose to take.

After my hit blog post about my fake honeymoon, I had offers skyrocket. I was being offered more money by dozens of companies, and I could now make double the money in half the time. I chose to only work with brands I liked.

"So, where are we going for my birthday?" I asked my organizer, Priya. She insisted on setting up something for my party. We had made a few small friends here, mainly these two girls, Isabella and Maria, who taught a Spanish class, and figured we'd do something together. Priya wanted to go clubbing, but I didn't want to spend my birthday in a club. She agreed on something smaller.

Instead, we ended up at a small dinner together, then headed out to a Cocktail Bar.

"How are you liking Spain, Hannah?" Isabella asked as we sat at a table together, drinking beautiful, well-crafted cocktails. The scene around us was young, attractive people, and the music wasn't too loud like I knew a club would be. Isabella was sitting next to me, and with her thick, long, black hair and beautiful brown eyes, I wasn't sure if men were looking at me or her. I only hoped they were looking at her.

"It's stunning. Madrid was nice, but I love being close to a beach again," I admitted.

"I think we need a shot," Priya said. I shook my head in response, but she had already grabbed the group shots. Priya was trying to get me loaded for some reason, and it was working. One cocktail and one shot hit me hard since I hadn't drunk more than a glass of wine with dinner in a few weeks.

"It's your birthday, Hannah, meaning it's time to let loose," Maria said, handing me another cocktail with a grin. They were drinking with me but at a slower pace, and it seemed like they had a plan. Why were they trying to get me so drunk, anyway?

"Let's go dance somewhere," Isabella said, and it made sense now. I felt a little more than tipsy, and it was my birthday. I agreed, and Priya jumped up excitedly. We paid our tab at the bar before leaving, and suddenly, everything clicked together. The club we walked to was a block away, and Priya wanted to get me plastered and vulnerable.

I should've known. Priya loved dancing and clubbing. When we arrived at the packed club, I took a few shots of vodka before joining Priya, Isabella, and Maria on the dance floor. Isabella had given us tips before about being safe. Turns out that men who went to clubs in Spain could be just as shady as American men at clubs. We didn't take any drink that didn't get poured in front of us. We didn't stray far from each other, even as Maria and Isabella danced with men.

Priya, however, stayed with me. My back was to her chest, and we were swaying our hips in sync with our hands in the air.

"Are you having fun?" she shouted above the music, her mouth inches from my ear.

"Yeah," I shouted back. "But where's the surprise? Hopefully, it's not the club."

She laughed. "No, it's not. It's still coming."

We were interrupted by two young, nicely dressed men stopping in front of us and grinning. I didn't like the way their eyes roamed my body, and I stopped all movements.

"Are you and your friend available?" One of them, a blond with slicked-back hair, asked.

I felt Priya's body warmth be removed from my back, but the music was so loud that I couldn't hear her walk away. Why would she leave me? When it was quickly replaced by someone else, someone much taller, I was concerned. Had another man snuck up on me? Then I felt hands grip my hips. I was about to turn around and deck him in the nose, but then he spoke, and I froze.

"She's taken, so you can move along now." Even through the loud music and crowded room, I could hear Wyatt's voice. I should've known it was him when my head didn't even reach his chin. I took a deep breath, relieved it was someone I knew, even if I was mad at him.

"Let's get out of here," he suggested when I turned around to greet him. He had a smile on his face, one that was soft and genuine.

"But Priya," I said as he started to lead me out of the club with my hand engulfed by his.

"Will be fine," he answered. "Isabella and Maria have it covered. She planned it, after all."

I nodded, and I let him lead me out of the club, where we entered a car. He gave the driver an address I didn't recognize, and the driver took off.

"Where are we going?" I asked.

"You'll see," he answered, smirking.

"God, I hate surprises," I remarked, but he knew that already.

"Before we get there, I need to apologize. I shouldn't have reacted how I did in Florida. I should've trusted you instead of letting insecurity take over. The thing is…I've wanted you for years. I've known I've wanted you for years. But I had to sit back and watch you love my brother, and I was terrified I was going to have to do it all over again."

"You and your brother need to learn to communicate through your issues," I remarked.

"I know. I'm working on it, I promise. You have to look at how we were raised and the environment we grew up in. It's no excuse, but we're still unlearning the bad behavior we were taught growing up. Learning how to love when our parents couldn't show it without money. Brad may be a lost cause, but I'm not," he pleaded.

"You grew up in a home with two parents, love from several nannies, and everything you could ask for. I grew up in a different world and ended up the opposite of both of you."

We arrived at our destination, and the car stopped outside a cute, skinny, stone, six-story tall apartment building. I had toured it before, so I knew they were stunning inside. Wyatt must have rented one for his trip.

He typed in a code to get inside the building and brought us inside to a stunning, modern apartment filled with white decorations and walls and dark brown accents throughout. Priya and I chose a more traditional style that was still beautiful, but this reminded me of home.

"Where are we?" I questioned.

"My new apartment," he answered, walking into the kitchen and opening the fridge. I took a seat at his marble-top kitchen island on a shockingly comfortable bar stool. "Want a drink?"

I nodded my head. "I should probably have some water, though I really want a drink of vodka right about now to process this. It's a good thing I'm already somewhat drunk."

He chuckled. "Sorry about that. Priya thought you'd take my presence better if she plied you with alcohol." So that was her actual plan all along. "She planned this all herself for your birthday. I'm your surprise."

"So, why do you have an apartment in Spain, exactly?" I questioned, drinking the water he set in front of me.

"Because, I moved here. I saw your post shortly after you made it. Brad brought it to my attention. I wanted to find you, but I had to stay back to formulate a plan. Someone offered to buy the practice from me earlier, and I refused. Now, I sold it to him, and we solidified our deal. I rented this place then planned my move after calling Priya and begging for her help."

I stood up from my seat, walking to close the distance between us before I realized what I was doing. "And why did Priya, my best friend for two decades, give in to your begging?"

"Because I told her I love you," he said in a soft voice, his hand brushing a piece of my hair behind my ear.

"You…what?" I questioned. I spent weeks believing he didn't want me. That he thought I wasn't good enough after all. Here he was, telling me three words I never thought I'd hear from him.

"I love you, Hannah Delayne," he answered again, pressing a kiss to my forehead. "I have for years."

I blinked a few times, processing his words. "But you love your job and Chicago. Chicago is your home."

"Chicago was where I was raised, but home is wherever you are. I want to be around you. I can be a doctor in more than just the States, or I can just be the guy dating the travel influencer if that's what you want."

"I don't want you to give up your dreams for me, just like you advised me." I frowned. I didn't want Wyatt to resent me like Brad did. I'd never be the girl who settled down in the States, didn't travel, and worked an office job. I'd never be the submissive wife. And I only hoped that was good enough for him to want, too.

"I'm not giving up my dreams, Hannah. I'm moving myself to follow my new dream. Being a doctor was never a dream. It was just something I did because I was good at it, and it'd make me money. I saved enough money that I didn't even need to work, which was why I worked so hard. And I sold for a seven-figure number. I'm set. I can live anywhere on this planet or the next as long as I'm by your side."

I let his words sink in before responding, accepting everything he told me. "I love you, too, Wyatt."

"Say it again," he whispered, pulling my body taut against his. A smile formed on my lips.

"I love you, Wyatt. Throughout our small times together, our little breakthroughs, I developed something for you that I couldn't understand. It was my mind recognizing that you were the better choice for me. Recognizing that you respected me, my job, and everything I wanted in life. If I could go back and change the outcome of that cafeteria day, I would."

"I don't have a ring, and this is impulsive, but will you marry me, Hannah? We can go buy whatever ring you want tomorrow. We can host whatever ceremony you want and go wherever you want for the honeymoon. I just want to marry you, and I want to be by your side forever. I want to travel together, make new memories, and do new things worldwide. I haven't wanted anyone else for five years and never will."

His eyes searched mine for an answer. I started to cry, a first for me while being proposed to.

"Don't cry, baby, please," he said, wrapping his arms around me and bringing me to his chest. My tears were wiped up by his shirt.

"They're happy tears," I said. "Of course, I'll marry you, Wyatt." Some would say we were crazy, but I knew I wanted to be with him. Marriage was just dating but with a legally binding contract. And assets. I trusted him with every bone in my body and with my heart.

"Maybe this time, we can have a joint bachelor and bachelorette party. Not in Nashville, though," he said with a smile, referencing our mishap in Nashville. It seemed so far away from now, but it wasn't that long ago. It was when my mind began questioning everything, but I couldn't process it at the time.

"Or we can just say fuck tradition," I offered instead.

He chuckled. "Agreed. I'm not a free man, and I only want to celebrate my impending wedding with you."

Chapter Forty-One

Hannah, Six Months Later

"I can't believe you've convinced two of my sons to marry you. You ruined one, and it wasn't enough," Wyatt's mother, Carol, said as she appeared behind me. I sighed, done with her bullshit by now. I told Wyatt we should give her a chance, but I was wrong. She deserves nothing. I opened my mouth to respond, but before I could speak, Wyatt was in the doorway of the hotel room.

"Mother, it was Hannah who suggested we give you a chance to be here. Respect her, or get the fuck out of here," Wyatt demanded. He was the picture of calm perfection as he leaned against the doorway, his arms crossed. He was in his suit, defending me in a way Brad never did, cementing my choice to marry him.

Carol looked like she was going to speak, but instead, she decided against it as she headed out the door. I was unsure whether it was to take her seat or return to her home in Chicago.

"You're not supposed to see me in my wedding dress," I remarked as he stepped closer, closing the distance between us. He placed his hands on my hip, pulling my body against his. Being in his arms felt like home, and now I'd get to be there forever. Or until he got sick of me and wanted a divorce.

"You forget we're eloping anyways, and you're not being walked down an aisle. We're about to go outside to our ceremony, and I would've seen you immediately," he pointed out, rolling his eyes.

I smiled as he lowered his head and closed his eyes, our lips meeting in a gentle kiss. I still got butterflies every time he kissed me, and my heart leaped when he smiled at me. His smile was so handsome, and for five years, I got to see it so little.

"I can't wait to marry you in front of seven people," I said. It was true. People thought I liked flashy things because of my job, but I didn't. I wanted to present myself in a more realistic manner to my friends and followers; show them the truth behind me.

With Brad, we had a large wedding planned with family, friends, and influencers that I hardly knew. It wasn't what I wanted. Brad was the one that wanted to make a spectacle out of our wedding. He told me it was what I should be doing as a successful influencer, and I went along with it because I figured he always had my best interest at heart. He told me that he had my best interest at heart so many times that I eventually believed it

With Wyatt, we agreed on a small elopement ceremony in Spain, where we moved to, then a honeymoon trip to Greece - where we wouldn't use our phones to do any work. Technically, Wyatt was an influencer now, too. My followers loved him. Everyone wanted an inside look at my real honeymoon, but they'd have to deal with the content from our first honeymoon together, even if it was fake. We wanted this time to be private for both of us.

If you told me over a year ago that I'd be going on a two-week honeymoon without my phone, I wouldn't believe it, but here I was. Nor did I think I'd have a small elopement ceremony, or be marrying Wyatt and not Brad. I had become a more private person that didn't feel the need to showcase so much of my life online anymore.

Our ceremony was held on Nova Icària Beach in Barcelona. It was one of the quieter beaches with fewer tourists. Watching the ceremony was Priya, who was documenting it for my social media pages, Brad, Wyatt's mom and dad, Adam, and Stacy. The person performing our wedding was a giddy Melissa. She had finally made it to Spain and wanted the honor of marrying us, since she said she knew we were destined to be together.

"I, Hannah DeLayne, take Wyatt Maverick to be my lawfully wedded husband, to have and to hold from this day forward, for better or worse, for richer or poorer, in sickness and in health, to love and to cherish, till death do us part," I vowed at Melissa's request.

When Wyatt repeated his vows, his mom visibly cringed, but even she couldn't distract me and take away my happiness. I was finally marrying the right man. The man that supported me all along, even from afar. Tomorrow, we'd head to a place neither of us had been before and start our life together. Wyatt and I agreed that we'd start our family immediately, and it wouldn't slow down our travels. We'd be a traveling family together. My followers had grown by a couple hundred thousand since my story first broke with Wyatt, and people followed us to keep up with how things ended up.

I guess reading about a girl failing to have her highly-anticipated wedding, then fucking his brother on their honeymoon, was something people loved to read about. I had offers for us to appear on television, and offers for us to interview with major magazines.

"Now, kiss her already!" Melissa said with joy, skipping the traditional language. It was why we went with a custom officiant versus a traditional one. Wyatt took me into his arms and brought his lips to mine, bringing me in for a kiss so deep you'd think we were alone.

"Okay, now stop," Priya teased. "You're not alone." We pulled apart and laughed together before leaving our ceremony together as a newlywed couple.

The best part about marrying Wyatt was the fact that I planned everything. I tried to get his input on where we should elope, where we should honeymoon, but he said he wanted it all on me. It was nice to be asked rather than be told. I didn't even have to answer to his mother once. Wyatt told her it was my way and we wouldn't change anything to meet her demands.

Once we headed to the small reception, we were hugged by the few people who attended our ceremony. Priya and Melissa hugged me the longest, bouncing up and down with joy for me. I hadn't seen Priya this happy when I was engaged to Brad, and she helped organize that.

"Hey, Hannah," Brad said quietly. I turned to find him standing behind me, rubbing his head. I blinked at him a few times. He was only here at his brother's request. He had always wanted his brother to see him get married, but I think he wanted Brad here to show that he was marrying *me*. He won me, and he treated me right.

"Hey, Brad," I responded coldly.

"I...I'm really sorry for what I did back in college. And for cheating on you instead of talking to you when I was lonely." He sounded genuine in his apology. "Congratulations on marrying my brother. You both deserve it," he said before walking away.

Truthfully, I was happy he cheated on me. It gave me the chance to find Wyatt, my true love. He had the opportunity to find the girl he genuinely wanted - Nicole. She wasn't phased by the fact that he chose me over her repeatedly. She was beautiful and wanted to be pampered and spoiled by him while staying home and raising children. Real ones this time, not the one she pretended to be pregnant with.

Due to Nicole coming from wealth, his mom loved her. After all, she chose to pretend to be pregnant to drive me away.

"Let's try to stay more sober than the last wedding night, okay?" Wyatt said as he approached me, joking. He wrapped his arm around my waist and pulled me close to him. "Tomorrow, we'll start making our daughter."

Priya faked a gag while Melissa beamed with joy.

"I can't wait," I replied with a wink.

"You guys gross me out with your sexual innuendos and the fact that you're so cute together," Priya pouted.

"You've got Spain all to yourself for the next week. Time to go find yourself a Spanish man, babe," I told her, grabbing her shoulder and laughing. "You never know what could happen in a week," I said, referencing my and Wyatt's relationship. We wouldn't be together if we hadn't taken a week-long vacation together - which was supposed to be my honeymoon.

I turned to Wyatt, looking at him with a cocked head as everyone else faded into the background. "You never told me what I said to you that night. What changed your mind."

He chuckled. "You said that you might have been about to marry the wrong brother. Drunk you was right, but we've rectified that situation now," he answered, bringing me into his arms in one swift motion and kissing me deeply in front of our cheering guests.

Chapter Forty-Two

Hannah

I wasn't nervous the first time I flew with Wyatt to my honeymoon destination. The second time around, I was. It was my official honeymoon with him this time, and we'd spend two weeks with each other, alone, and not including the internet. I had never given up work for that long. I had never been on a real honeymoon before. I had never even spent two weeks alone with a man. To top it all off, I had never been to Santorini. We chose to stay in the popular, gorgeous destination of Fira.

When Wyatt told me I could choose where we went on our honeymoon, my first thought was Greece. I wanted to go somewhere I had never been before and do it while taking our social media break. I planned to fully immerse myself in the experience, rather than document it for strangers online.

Our suite was better than I could have ever imagined. My jaw dropped when we walked into our room with a private terrace with an infinity pool. We had a beautiful view of the ocean and other parts of the city. Cliffs surrounded the oceans and added beauty to the view. The weather was sunny, warm, and bright, which was incredibly welcoming.

We chose Fira for the epic caldera sunset views, which were raved about by many. If we wanted, Oia was a twenty-minute bus ride away and allegedly had more restaurants and outdoor activities. We planned a lot of poolside hangouts, sex, dining, and outdoor adventures.

We promised to do an ATV tour, a hike around the island, a private tour, and another dinner cruise with views of the city and the caldera. Choosing someone who wanted to put my choices above his was nice, but I couldn't make it all about me. Wyatt chose the activities, and I agreed. They all sounded fun to me, and he knew me enough to know what we'd enjoy doing together. We wanted to make a point of doing things we didn't normally do in Spain.

I jumped onto my back on the bed, and Wyatt climbed on top of me. "You made a good choice," Wyatt praised. "Now, when do we get to start making a child?"

I laughed, hitting him in the chest and jokingly shoving him off of me. I stood up, looking down at him. I bit my lip when the nerves of what I was about to say took over. "If we have a daughter like we both want, can we name her Leah? It was my mom's middle name. I want to honor her in some way."

Wyatt stood, placing his hands on either of my arms and rubbing lightly. He leaned down and kissed my forehead. "Of course. But only if I get to name our child if they're a boy or when we have a boy," he bargained.

I nodded. I knew when the time came, Wyatt wouldn't pick a name without consulting me. And he'd never name his child after his dad or brother.

"Now, let's get in that damn pool," I announced, sprinting towards our outdoor terrace. I kicked off my sandals before we got outside, then tore off my shirt and slid off my shorts. We previously confirmed that our balcony was private, and the walls prevented people from being able to see us. Wyatt was further behind me, trying to remove his clothes as quickly as I could. I stripped down to nothing, but before I could willingly enter the pool, Wyatt snuck up behind me and scooped me into his arms. He spun me around while I held onto his neck, sending me into a fit of laughter.

He walked into the pool from the steps, forcing me into the water with him. We were both naked and once we were in the pool, he let me stand on my own feet. We walked to the edge of the pool to overlook the ocean, which was such a stunning sight. I was glad we had this all to ourselves rather than sharing with hundreds of guests like we did in Florida. Plus, the ocean view beats a lake view any day.

It was getting close to sunset outside, and beautiful hues of yellow and pink overtook the sky. He swam up behind me, placing his hands on my hips and pulling my back to his chest. I could feel his erection on my backside, and I knew I was blushing. The view was stunning, and the pool was private, but what we were doing still felt scandalous and unlike myself.

He pushed my hair onto one shoulder and kissed my neck a few times before biting on the skin and gently sucking.

"I want to fuck you with this view," he said. His hands roamed my curves until they reached my breasts, where he lightly rubbed my nipples as they began to harden. I threw my head back, leaning against his chest as I gave in to the pleasure of his touch.

"What are you waiting for then, husband?"

With one hand teasing my nipple, the other trailed down my stomach and stopped between my thighs, lightly rubbing my clit. I jolted with pleasure at the new sensation. Wyatt smirked into my neck.

"Just waiting to get you ready for me, wife. A pool is a little harder to have sex in, but we can make it work. I want to create new experiences with you, including fucking in a terrace pool at sunset on a beautiful island."

I smiled and reached behind me to feel between us, taking his length in my hand and slowly giving him a few pumps. "I'm ready," I said breathily. I was impatient, and we had the perfect time with the sunset in view.

Wyatt lifted me by the hips, and I held on to the pool's edge. It wasn't hard since the weight and resistance changed in the water. I felt him line himself up at my entrance, and a second later, I felt him roughly push inside to the hilt. I wanted to grip something, but my arms were on concrete. "Fuck, I missed this feeling, baby," Wyatt said.

"It's only been a few days, babe," I pointed out but shut up when he pulled almost all the way out, then pushed inside again, hard. I was so full of lust that I couldn't formulate a thought anymore.

"A few days is too long without you." He built a slow, torturous pace, but each thrust sent him deep inside me. To make him hit at a different angle, I used my hips to push him further back and lifted my ass more. The move sent him deeper inside of me, and he groaned loudly.

I never thought I'd be the girl who craved sex so much, but I guess I didn't have a way to know what I was missing out on. Wyatt was everything I needed and more. And I had almost settled for less-than-mediocre sex for the rest of my life. I thought I might be asexual, but now I knew that wasn't true.

"Choke me," I requested. I hadn't asked him to do that before, but I knew he'd do just about anything I asked, including killing someone if I asked.

He didn't hesitate as one hand moved to the front of my throat, his fingers pressing into the sides without squeezing the front of my neck. My moans became louder and more frequent. The way he had me near orgasm, with his hand choking me and the other rubbing against my clit, had me seeing stars at the edge of my vision.

"Do you like that, Hannah?" he asked. I almost couldn't respond to how good I felt. I was so focused on the way he was pounding into me and sending jolts of pleasure through my body.

"Y-yes," I croaked through my choked throat. "You feel so fucking good."

"I wish you could see what I see when I'm fucking you. You're so fucking gorgeous, and you take me so fucking well. There's an island and an ocean behind you, and you're still the most beautiful thing in my view."

He pinched my clit lightly, and I squirmed, causing him to press harder on my throat as he held my body against his. Once I was still, his grip loosened again. He stopped his movements and pulled out of me, removing both hands. I pouted at the loss of him, but he quickly remedied the situation by turning me over to face him. He placed his hands under my thighs and lifted me, pushing himself back inside of me to the hilt. I let out a loud moan as he unexpectedly filled me again.

"I needed to see you while you fell apart with my touch."

My back was against the pool. One of his hands was between us, rubbing my clit again. His other hand tangled in my hair and gently pulled my hair near my scalp. I thought it would hurt, but it felt really good, almost like I was getting a head massage. With his hand gripping my hair, he pulled my head towards his and pressed his lips against mine in a deep, searing kiss. His tongue licked the seam of my lips, and I let him in. Then they ferociously moved together as his kiss swallowed my moans.

He broke the kiss and pressed his forehead to mine. His lips parted, and he let out a few moans. "Fuck, Hannah, you're mine. You were made for me, baby."

With him saying I was his, I shattered. The orgasm that had been slowly building suddenly ripped through me intensely, and his thrusts were slower and deeper while I rode out the wave of pleasure. He brought me into a kiss once more as his movements stilled, and he released himself inside of me. I felt the way my pussy gripped him as he squeezed every last drop inside of me.

Wyatt left the pool and told me to wait, then came back a minute later with a towel for me. He guided me out of the pool in my post-orgasm haze and wrapped a towel around me. Our terrace had a patio sofa, and we sat on it together as he wrapped me in his arms and cuddled me. The sun was close to setting, and I couldn't imagine a better way to kick off our first real honeymoon.

Chapter Forty-Three

Wyatt

We spent two weeks doing everything we planned and more. We hiked around the island more than once, walking to the neighboring village of Oia a few times. We grabbed food while we were there, then took the bus back. I even brought her to a restaurant with a sunset ocean view, and sunset viewing happened to become our new favorite thing on the island. I'm not sure if it was because of what happened the first night or just because we ended up watching the sunset from somewhere new every night.

We tried to stick to primarily Greek cuisine and were doing well. We tried new food together, and it was a fun experience, even if we didn't like everything we tried. Sometimes, Hannah felt sick after eating, too. She hadn't thrown up yet, though. We ate the same meals, too, and I felt fine.

After a week of hiking and sunsets, we decided to rent an ATV to get around the island for fun. She made me drive and held me tightly as we drove throughout the island during the day. We visited new places and even found a few beaches together. We even watched a sunset from a hill's peak on the ATV together.

"Do you think you want to live in Spain forever?" I asked her as we sat up on the hill. We hadn't talked about where we saw our future beyond being together. I'd follow her wherever, and I ensured she knew that before we married. She could tell me she wanted to move to Ohio tomorrow, and I wouldn't protest.

"Part of me has always wanted to live in Germany. Maybe Berlin or Munich," she admitted.

"And you know they're landlocked with no beaches, right?" I teased. She hit me in the chest and laughed.

"Yes, silly. I don't always need to be near a beach. They're beautiful, but I can still travel to one. I want to grow up somewhere where our kids will have the best opportunities, a safe life, and a secure future. Which is why we can't go back to the States," she joked, but she was right. We both knew that it wasn't the same raising the kids there as in Europe. Hannah was never meant to stay in one place forever, and she certainly wasn't meant to live in Chicago forever like Brad wanted. With me, she could be whomever she wanted to be, and I'd support her.

"Germany is beautiful, has incredible worker rights, healthcare, and a great education system. I think we'd be lucky to live there one day," I told her. I wanted her to make choices, knowing I'd follow her anywhere and do anything for her, but she needed to know that I'd go along with what she wanted for her to feel comfortable. Since I knew that about her, I made sure sometimes to make it seem like things were my idea so she'd go along with them. Sure, I was cheating the system, but making her happy was worth it.

We returned to Spain, and the chaos of work caught up with us. We had Priya communicating with people while we were away, but there were things she specifically saved for us, too. Our first plan with Priya was to make a post with one of our wedding photos, and it was one of the most liked photos we ever posted.

We had a few brand videos to make together and a few calls with different companies. Hannah wasn't feeling well since she caught a bug on the trip, so I stepped up to the plate and took care of our work duties and of her. I brought her soup in bed, got her anti-nausea medication, and rubbed her feet. Thankfully, she made a doctor's appointment the week after we returned. Despite her getting ill toward the end, we had a great time.

I drove Hannah to her doctor's appointment, and the doctor gave her a few tests. There was one specifically that I asked for, just as a precaution. When the doctor came back, she was all smiles. "Well, I've got good news for you both," she said. We stared at her in anticipation. "You're going to be parents!"

Hannah looked as pale as a ghost. "Holy shit, I'm pregnant?" she asked.

"Baby, are you okay?" I checked on her, waving a hand in front of her eyes. She looked in shock.

"I didn't think it would be that fast. Our honeymoon *just* ended," she admitted. I think the surprise got to her more than the idea of having a kid. She wanted kids, so I knew she wasn't upset about being pregnant.

"We'll send you to get an ultrasound for more information, but for now, how long has it been since your last period?"

Hannah thought to herself for a moment, then her eyes widened. "Six weeks. I didn't even notice. I had just been on birth control for so long. I was used to not always having a period."

"I told you birth control would stop working fast. You insisted you had been on it too long," Wyatt teased.

"You're roughly six weeks pregnant, and we'll confirm that with an ultrasound. Then, I'll set you up with an OB-GYN in the area. Congratulations, you two," the doctor said before walking outside.

"Holy shit, babe, we're going to be parents. It's actually happening," she said, a smile finally appearing on her face. "Little Leah, or…" she said, looking at me for the potential male name.

"Baby Bartholomew," I answered with a wink.

"We'll work on that. We have a while."

Epilogue

Hannah

Since Priya still worked for Wyatt and me, three years later, we still lived in Barcelona together. Last year, Priya finally met someone. We went out to eat at a new place that opened up, and there, she met the chef. He took to her immediately, coming to our table to speak to her. Now, they had just moved in together a few weeks ago, and we decided to celebrate with a dinner gathering. Brad and Nicole were flying in to join us since we hadn't seen them for Leah's first birthday.

Lorenzo, Priya's boyfriend, was a chef at a famous restaurant downtown that we had eaten at once. Due to his connections, he got us a reservation at the second hottest spot in the city, which was booked for six months. We got a nice spot in a corner, and Wyatt and I arrived first. Our babysitter was watching Leah tonight, then we'd go out with Brad and Nicole and explore the city with her tomorrow. Brad loved his niece, and they Facetimed a lot.

Nicole lightened up once I married Wyatt, leaving Brad to her. She felt more secure and no longer saw me as a threat. Sometimes, she still acted like she had this incredible prize that she tore away from me. Overall, I won. I had Wyatt, and he was better for me like Brad was better for Nicole. Since she was the future step-aunt to Leah, I put aside my differences to welcome her into the family.

After all, she was pregnant with Brad's child. Six months from now, Leah would have a cousin.

"So, we've got something to announce," Brad said first, standing at the table holding Nicole's hand. He smiled at her before announcing, "We're moving to Munich."

Great, my ex would be moving to where we planned to end up next year. Maybe Wyatt had talked to Brad about it, since we were family after all. At least Leah would have her cousin nearby, and Wyatt would have his brother. Wyatt jumped up from his seat and ran to hug his brother.

"We're happy to have you guys," I said with a small smile. Priya gave me a knowing glance. "What's happening with the company then?" I asked, referencing his dad's company that he took over when he retired a few years ago.

"Regional headquarters. Steve is taking over our Chicago office, and I'm expanding to Germany and opening an office there. Already got all the permits and visas I need," Brad said proudly.

"We've got something to say, too," Priya said, gathering everyone's attention. One day, we'd get to say our news, too. "We're engaged!" she beamed, jumping up from her seat and showing off the ring we somehow missed. Lorenzo put a solid rock on her finger, and Priya deserved it all. She was beautiful, fun, smart, and never fully appreciated until he came around.

"Good, because you're going to be fired with a hefty severance package," I finally announced. "I'm going down to a small, part-time influencer role since we've saved so much over the past few years. I really want to focus on fun memories with my family, and Wyatt is going to spend a few months providing free care for a charity in another country. We're going to follow him, then, when our child is due, we're going to…move to Munich," I said with a sigh.

Priya's eyes widened. "But I love my job," Priya pouted.

"Well, now it's time to enjoy your life with your fiancé and maybe start being an influencer yourself. You've started to gain followers from my tags, Priya. You're gorgeous, and they love you and your fun, quirky personality," I reminded her. She was gorgeous, and all of my followers knew it. With her long, dark hair and her skin that was several shades darker than mine, and her big, doe eyes, she was a favorite on my page.

"I never thought about it that way, but you're right, I should," she said with a firm smile.

Since the money dramatically increased over the past few years, with my actual wedding and the birth of our child, I had saved over seven figures. I planned to drastically decrease my posting and lower the number of sponsorships and brand deals, and we'd still have enough to get by. Living in another country was shockingly more affordable than I expected compared to living in Chicago.

"I truly never imagined life turning out this way for all of us, but now I couldn't imagine it any other way," I said to the group. We held up our champagne flutes and clinked our classes before taking a drink together. They didn't know that mine was a sparkling non-alcoholic drink. We were one big, unconventional, happy family. "Oh, we're welcoming baby number two in seven months," I announced.

9 781088 253434